HYPERCAPITALISM

AND OTHER TALES OF PLANETARY MADNESS

ANDRÉS VACCARI

WANTON SUN

Published in 2023 by Wanton Sun
Melbourne, Australia
www.wantonsun.com

ISBN 978-0-6456543-3-2

Cover by Matthew Revert.
Typesetting by Wanton Sun.

'American Djinn' first appeared in *Overland* #210 (2013). 'The Shadows and the Swarm' first appeared in *Alchemy: Visible Ink* 11 (2000). 'I Will Never Leave You', 'The Life Next Door' and 'Cooling Down' first appeared in *El enjambre y las sombras* (EMB 2017). 'Arrivals/Arribos' first appeared in *Australian Latino Press* (2015). 'End of Season' first appeared in *Amorphik: An Erotic Constellation* (Sub Dee Industries, 1999). '"The Consortium must die," the suicide ghost said' first appeared in *Light and Dark* #5 (2018). 'Becoming' first appeared in *Burak* (2022). 'Hypercapitalism: A Future Memoir' is based on 'Rotting in the Office', originally published in *Roadworks* #5 (1999). 'Welcome Day' and 'The Forest' are previously unpublished.

To my mother Diana and father Jorge,
who always encouraged and supported
me in my scribblings, with love.

CONTENTS

AMERICAN DJINN

Day 1: Aljazhab

The oldest city in the world seems a likely place to find ghosts.

The cab plunges into a hot, dusty turmoil of traffic, crowds and distorted calls to prayer. After the flight over, and five hours of sensory deficit, the city wakes me with a slap to the face. The smells stream inside: rose tobacco, rank sewage, spicy charred lamb from street stands. The light has a peculiar quality. It crystallises in the torpid mist of exhaust vapours and sand, making everything at once dream-like and more real.

The city's outskirts conserve the drabness that would have been called modern in the late 1970s, but beauty is gradually unveiled as we enter. The town is an incongruent palimpsest of materials and styles. Asphalt mixes with glazed mosaic, plaster with stone, stucco with plastic. The advertising signs seem time-tunnelled from another era—and so do I. It's been twelve years and Aljazhab is as I remember it, yet there's a sense of displacement, as though I've been dumped into an elaborate reconstruction of that memory.

Amorites, Hittites, Akkadians, Phoenicians, Assyrians, Persians, Greeks, Romans, Arabs, Crusaders, Ottomans. The United States of America is the last in a long line of infamous empires that ruled this place during the last 8000 years. The French seized it, briefly, in the early twentieth century, before the bloody uprisings that led to the modern state of Qiram. At the peak of their powers, each empire must have seemed invincible and eternal, but now look at them. Their remains are barely decipherable in the scatter of eroded architectural motifs. I'm certain that the ghosts of the Americans will eventually drown in the din of this primeval, overpopulated netherworld. But can the undead die a second death?

My Arabic is rusty and Yassar, the driver, plasters the gaps in our conversation with spurts of English. He lets the taxi drive itself while punctuating his comments with vehement hand movements. As the walls of the ancient citadel loom into view, the difference between road and sidewalk, shaky at best, vanishes altogether. The driver curses at a cluster of Suzuki vans stuck in a narrow intersection in front of us. These comical relics, retrofitted with electric engines, are popular for being cheap and small enough to negotiate the narrow maze of backstreets in the old town.

We slow down to a human pace and Yasssar's gaze hovers on the rear-view mirror. He asks me what I'm doing in Aljazhab and I answer as honestly as I can.

'I'm curious.'

He nods to himself and for a moment appears to stifle laughter, but then he turns serious.

'Go to the main square, my friend. Go to the central bus station. You'll see the real ghosts there. Children burned with the chemical weapons, grandmothers without legs, everyone begging and dying.'

The unmanned wheel shudders as we rush through a gap in the chaos. Yassar is making me inexplicably nervous, and I feel I must prove something to him. Perhaps I need to show him I'm not American, or maybe I need to justify my visit.

'I'm a journalist. It's my profession. See, I was working for Associated Press last time, covering the last days of the invasion. And I was one of the few to openly call it that—*invasion*—although that bit was mostly edited out.'

But Yassar has lost all interest. At the hotel, he glances at my twenty-sheikh note against the dusty light from the windscreen and quickly pockets it. I'm fresh from the plane, after all.

'May Allah give you plenty of children.'

Too late for that, my friend.

Day 3

Khaled says he'll meet me at the old Sheraton tomorrow evening, which is fine since the feeling of displacement hasn't worn off.

I walk around the edge of the moat of the ancient citadel, too anxious to go in. It seems that the desecration of history can make me angrier than the killing of thousands of people. The historical heart has been carefully reconstructed and the new brickwork melds seamlessly with the old materials, but I know that most of it is fake. Everywhere, I see the same desire to patch things up, to leave the past behind. After all, glorifying the ancient past is one of President Ahmed al-Zhara's main strategies for facing the future.

The Sheraton has been renamed Mehmunkhuneh Qasr, which means 'Hotel Castle', in reference to the nearby medieval ruins. Back then, it was my home for nearly a year. Now it's hardly recognisable. The whole place has been wallpapered anew with filigreed Arabic patterns in gold, turquoise and brown. Photos of al-Zhara are prominent in the lobby and reception area, and I see his smiling, waving portrait everywhere in the city.

A Sunni Muslim, like most of Qiram, al-Zhara traded his status as the poster boy of al-Qaeda's anti-US resistance for political profit. Now, he's going for more, remaking himself as a beacon of pan-Arabic unity in a region of shaky democracies, fragile peace deals, constant civil war and ancient, irreconcilable faiths. The American collapse and the near annihilation of Israel brought no visible improvement to the welfare of the average Arab or Persian citizen, but it's early days, so everyone says. Al-Zhara's family owns a construction company that got most of the post-war contracts. On the bright side, he's weaned the economy from its dependence on oil and steered it towards renewable energies. They say he's an example for the region, but the truth is complicated.

The concierges wear dark suits and chequered keffiyehs. They have the acquiescent, cheerful manner of air stewards. This is one of the few places in the city where alcohol is legally obtainable. I remember the feverish atmosphere during the time of the transition, the swarm of journalists and officials, the abrupt outbursts of violence.

Sometimes (not often nowadays), I'm woken in the middle of the night by the sound of an explosion in my head. It takes me a whole hour to go back to sleep. Once, the insurgents managed to launch a bomb into a window on the first floor, killing five people. I'm not sure where the explosions in my head come from, whether it's Assam, Kashmir or Tripoli. I'd seen dead bodies before but never twitching like in Aljazhab. Like they wanted to get up and away from there.

In the unconscious of the world, time heals nothing.

Day 5

Last night Khaled finally arrived and watched me drink at the bar of the hotel. The beers are Japanese, the wine Saudi Arabian, the whiskey Irish. Khaled is a British-educated doctor, born in Syria and now living in Baghdad. I first met him fifteen years ago, after the bombing of Tehran, when he worked for Al Jazeera. Some dark twists of fate made him become a reporter. Most of his family was killed in Damascus and he felt he had a duty to record the American atrocities. He started off embedded as an army doctor on the side of the resistance.

We spent six months working here together. Khaled has put on weight and grown a beard, but otherwise it seems like no time has passed. Family bonds grow between people in such circumstances. After a lengthy and effusive welcome, Khaled pelts me with questions about the Hague trials, the polar winter, the water shortage, the secessions in the US. But I tell him there is no more to know than what you see on the news. Besides, reality is so much more interesting when you have footage.

A freelance bum, he calls me. He pronounces it *bom*. 'The whole world is the Third World now.' He belly laughs as though he invented that cliché. His gaze narrows. 'You're blogging this, aren't you? I've checked. Don't mention I'm fat.'

He glances furtively at the scars on my face. I lift my chin to show him the latest one on my neck. He inspects it with a professional frown, shaking his head.

'You white people chose the worst spots to colonise. You should have stayed in Europe. Really.'

'And miss out on all that gold, cheap real estate and exotic two-headed women? We would do it all over again if we had to. Anyway, it worked quite well for you in the end. You Arabs are sitting at the top of the food chain. Again.'

When the conversation begins to deflate, we're left with no choice but to face the reason for our meeting. We're both kind of embarrassed at first, although I have the advantage of being half drunk. We spread out what we have on the table. I have maps, mainly. He has photographs and reports. We compare facts and intel. The first sightings were reported six years ago in Iraq. At first, the Iraqis assumed US covert operations were being carried out in their country, which was ridiculous, of course. I heard the

Iraqis sent reconnaissance missions. The UN team and the air surveys yielded nothing but a handful of blurry photographs that can be easily Googled. They could be of anything.

The reports continued to spread across Iran, Syria, Qiram and other former foci of the doomed US takeover. These shadowy figures became part of the local folklore, adding to the already abundant stock of ghost stories in these parts. Apparently, they can be seen only at dusk, during sandstorms or in heavy haze, and they appear and vanish suddenly, like mirages. Silent explosions can be seen flaring up in the night. Some people have claimed that, after sunset, they hear distant gunfire and fighter jets flying overhead. In some villages, people are afraid to go out at night or let their children play in the streets.

'These are straight from the source.' Khaled shows me a photo of what appears to be a human shadow advancing through a sandstorm, the shape of a soldier crowned by the distinct Advanced Combat Helmet. The grainy image has been blown up. 'It's a *doozy*. Is that what you Australians call it? It's fair dinkum, this one.' I try to seem amused.

'Whatever we do,' he says, 'we need to stay away from the border. Zionist terrorists are active all along the frontiers with Jordan, Israel and Lebanon. I can accompany you for three days. Then I must go to my cousin's wedding in Damascus, and you're on your own for a week. Supposedly I'm back at work then, but I'll do my best to come back and check on you.'

'I appreciate it.'

'Just keep me out of the credits. That's all I ask.'

'This is just preliminary research. Won't harm your reputation.'

'You've sold out to this New Gonzo stuff now. No one will believe you. Who is it, The History Channel?'

'I'll know the buyer when I have the product.'

Khaled flicks the corner of the photograph with his ring finger. His expression darkens. 'I don't doubt that these mirages are a product of the imagination, but why do they take just *this* shape?

If this is some weird way to cope with collective trauma, then we Arabs must be really masochistic.'

But the reports might have a source. During the final stage of the American collapse, as supplies dwindled and the command structure crumbled from Washington downwards, bands of soldiers went AWOL and looted local villages and towns, raping and killing whoever stood in their way. These episodes joined the long list of war crimes that American officials, including two ex-presidents, are answering for at The Hague.

I tap my finger on a spot on the map: Umm Jebel, a former US base in the nomad routes. Khaled shrugs. 'Time for one last round?' he says, pointing to my empty glass, reading my mind.

Day 6: Umm Jebel

We set off into the desert at the first glimmer of dawn, narrowly missing prayer time. With its smart temperature management and silky hydrogen engine, Khaled's 4WD is like a biosphere on wheels. Once we cut through the hills northwest of Aljazhab and hit the H1, we enter a flat, eerie, golden emptiness. It takes my mind a few long minutes to tune in and appreciate the eventfulness of this landscape.

To a Westerner's mindset, the desert is an unforgiving nothingness, but to the people who live here, this place teems with information. Every sand dune is a sign and every mudflat a story. It's obvious to me why the religions of the Book are the religions of the desert, cults of an angry Father who has withdrawn from sight and left his children to wander alone in a world without end. I'm careful not to share these thoughts with Khaled, although he would probably just laugh at my ignorance.

This highway has seen a lot of action, years of routine sabotaging, hijacking and bombings, yet it looks fresh and perfectly smooth, another indication that post-war Qiram is good business if you know where to find it.

Soon we are passing through a series of oases. It takes us five minutes to drive through the largest one. These patches of bright-green vegetation, dotted with clusters of palm trees, are springing out everywhere, fertile areas locking in the moisture and slowly spreading. Khaled tells me that the rainy season has just started. I open the window and the gust of humid, almost tropical heat takes me by surprise. In another twenty years, this place will be unrecognisable.

Next, we drive past a sprawling wind farm, one of the largest in the region. It's set at some distance from the highway, accessible through a series of unmarked dirt tracks. We can just make out the tall, serene turbines sprouting from the landscape like a new, monstrous breed of flower. After two hours, we switch places and I take over the driving. We're both aware of the vague anxiety gathering around us. This is, after all, a place of voices and visions. The desert makes all those stories more plausible.

The sun is climbing fast, and we're slicing through curtains of heat. A mirror of scorching air hangs at the vanishing point on the horizon, apparently receding from us. I notice another difference since the last time I was here. Flat, horizontal rainbows are forming in the humid air, like floating mirages.

We arrive at Umm Jebel by ten. This was once an archae-ological site dating from the sixth century, but the Americans destroyed what little remained. Forward Operating Base Carson housed the 1st Infantry Division and the 3rd Armored Cavalry Regiment. It was a strategic resupply point between Aljazhab and the Syrian border. It housed a small airbase and was also the centre for highway security operations on the H1. Most of the major US bases have been looted to the last tent pole and what remained has been dismantled as part of al-Zhara's campaign of historical renewal, but some military emplacements have been overlooked or adapted to other purposes.

Following the GPS, we turn sharply into the sand and drive with blind faith in near-zero visibility. Khaled taps me on the arm, snapping me out of reverie. I take this as a sign to stop. Sure enough, the GPS shows our car standing on the destination icon.

As the sand clears, we find ourselves at the foot of a shallow artificial embankment. There's movement ahead: people waving at us and hurrying towards the car. The children arrive first, dressed in striking, many-coloured kaftans. Their vibrant, curious faces swarm around us as we leave the vehicle. They feel the threads on the tires with their fingertips, and they pat the slick grey glazing of the chassis.

We climb the embankment. We're standing on an old runway almost wholly covered in sand and rocks. Concrete slabs mark the old perimeter, but the fence is gone. Camp Carson has been stripped down to its garters. Fences, doors, containers, bricks, poles—everything that could be moved has been plundered. We approach the nomad constructions that meld ingeniously with the derelict, still-robust foundations and scaffolding. The rusty, sinking skeletons of two armoured vehicles flank the main entrance. The children are speaking all at once, a dialect I don't understand. They flash smiles. Khaled waves them away, but they press closer. For some reason, they find the whole situation hilarious. An old man approaches, dressed in an impeccable white kaftan and keffiyeh, carrying a long staff. He looks extraordinarily agile for his age, and I infer he is the sheikh of the tribe. He offers a wide, three-toothed smile and his arms open slightly in welcome.

We're led through the camp, past barking dogs, more curious children, groups of women with embroidered scarves and indigo tattoos, a bonfire of tamarisk and willow, wandering goats, and the smell of cardamom and roasting coffee. A group gradually accretes around us. The introductions and well-wishing are exhaustive.

They're speaking Arabic now, and I let Khaled do most of the talking. I'm amazed at how the nomads have taken advantage of the few remaining walls and structures. Wall coverings hang between steel beams and the concrete floors are dressed in goat-hair rugs.

Having streamlined the ancient art of occupation, the Americans assembled their bases quickly from prefab parts. They could erect long-term fortifications such as this in a matter of days. The old barracks have been converted into a stable for donkeys and horses, and I notice two camels, a sign that the clan is doing well. Most of the living quarters have been set inside the two medium-sized aircraft hangars, which keep cool during the day and warm at night. We are invited to sit on a carpeted floor under an awning. Five of the men join us, plus the sheikh who follows our conversation in silence at first.

With our first coffee and dates, Khaled broaches the subject of our visit and the conversation heats up. The term 'infidel djinn' crops up repeatedly. More people join us, speaking over one another, eyes sparkling and hands fluttering energetically.

They've been here six weeks. There are good pastures around, and the buildings provide seasonal shelter from rain, wind and storms, but when the sun hides, the lights and sounds often break the night: gunfire, distant helicopters, and sometimes wheezing drones overhead. The animals are frightened and can change course without warning.

'It's like they sense danger ahead,' one man says. 'They don't listen to us, and they see things we can't see.' Some of the animals even refuse to give milk.

It's not the first time they've encountered the djinn. Apparently, everyone in the desert is used to them, but they seem much worse around here. They're waiting for the rainy season to stop so they can move on.

I ask if anyone has seen the djinn close-up. 'Amr!' the sheikh exclaims. *Amr! Amr!* they all agree. Amr is promptly dragged out from somewhere among the tents. He is a youth of no more than eighteen, with a smooth, frightened face. He looks at me for a moment, uncomprehendingly, and the men nudge him to speak.

It happened shortly after the sunrise prayers. He was milking his father's goats when the animals started bawling and getting restless. As he turned to look behind him, he almost stepped into the apparition. Amr was very young when the US first invaded his country, but almost everyone in these parts recognises the iconic image of the American soldiers. It was one of them, he's certain of it. The soldier was tall and his face was white and glistening with sweat. He had a thick beard, and his uniform was tattered and filthy. The soldier held his rifle in a resting position, pointing down to his left, hugging the butt like it was his last tin of food.

He was looking at him. Amr emphasises the word because the soldier's eyes were hard to see. They were like holes through which Amr could see the red dusk light of the desert summer. He saw through the apparition's flesh, which seemed to be made of dust, like the shapes you spot in a cloud. Terrified, the boy sunk to his knees. Amr was sure he was going to die—it even occurred to him that he was already dead.

Then, as he pressed on the ground with his eyes tightly shut, he felt something cold brush past him—through him like a shiver. He prayed intensely for some time, and when he looked up the soldier was gone and his father was standing there, ready to reprimand him. Amr spent the following three days hiding in his tent.

Over lunch (a delicious lamb kapsa), people offer their testimony. Zulema, an elder, says that the infidels have been denied the afterworld and so are condemned to suffer in their own souls the pain they inflicted on the Arab people. Some of these men fought in the resistance and must be proud of their victory over the once-supreme American empire.

During those last, endless weeks, as the US troops beat a hasty and chaotic retreat, the insurgents took the fight to the streets of the villages. Low on food, ammunition and morale, bands of American soldiers roamed the desert and the roads, laying siege to villages and scavenging supplies, while the US government and media blamed the atrocities on sectarian warfare. Many troops succumbed to dehydration and delirium, while others were picked off one by one, some by the very hands that gesticulate in front of me now.

After lunch, I leave Khaled with the clan and wander through the camp, trying to stay in the shade. As I scan the distance, I find myself expecting to see a dead American, but it's too early and too still, and the desert stands timelessly in the searing air, impervious to anything.

Some children are following me. I recognise them from our welcoming committee. 'Are you American?' one asks in English. The faces gather around expectantly.

'No,' I say as emphatically as possible.

'You're looking for the djinn,' he says. The children appear excited rather than frightened by the notion of these ghosts, if indeed that's what they are. They lead me away into the heart of the ruins, where a pack of emaciated dogs (which look more like wolves) huddles in the shade. The children shout at them and, surprisingly, the dogs retreat obediently. The children reach a pile of debris and form a circle around it. I see nothing but ruins: broken bricks, shattered concrete, pieces of fibreglass and plastic sheeting, rusty pipes. And sand everywhere.

Behind half a brick wall standing in the wreck, the children have amassed their treasure. Under a canvas flap with burnt edges, dozens of helmets are carefully arranged in a pile. The children point to names and slogans scrawled on the side: ordinary names like Jones and Andrews; clichéd and obscene mottoes about victory, pussy, blood and death. They show me the rest of the collection: a handful of name tags; a pair of broken binoculars; Coca-Cola cans riddled with bullets; pens, boots, watches, water bottles.

Three of the youngest children stand guard some distance away. I gather their parents don't know about this. They watch carefully for my reaction, which is a mix of dismay and fascination. I promise them I won't say anything to the adults.

Although most of these children are too young to remember, they would've lost mothers, grandparents, uncles or other relatives during the invasion. To them, the American soldiers must be mythical creatures, dimly remembered, who once held power over life and death. And yet these monsters of legend can't harm them anymore. One of them, about ten years old, puts a helmet on and screws up his face. Attention, he shouts in thick English. *Kill! Kill!* The others find this hilarious.

Then a reverential silence falls on the group. Rummaging in the pile of remains, the oldest child unveils the most precious items in the collection: an eroded M4 carbine and a dusty SAM-R rifle with a crooked barrel. I notice with relief that the magazines are missing. Perhaps there are bullets in the chamber, yet I doubt they would work. The boy lifts the carbine carefully and shows it to me. Evidently, he's the only one authorised to touch it. The children aren't laughing now. They stare at the weapons with the awe reserved for religious objects.

The shadows lengthen around us. As we walk back to the encampment, the children recover their former merriment, laughing and trying to trip one another. I strike up a conversation with the one who showed me the weapons. As the hangars come into view, he asks if the Americans will come back.

I assure him that the soldiers are gone forever, that the tales about their ghosts roaming the desert are just that: tales. '*Insha'Allah*, they can't harm anybody.'

He seems happy to hear this and hops back to join the other children.

Day 10

Khaled is gone now, and things are rather lonely. I've been working on the material we've gathered, which doesn't add much to what we already had. Amr's story is the closest we've come to encountering the American djinn. I believed him, I believed those eyes, yet that alone won't make it more authentic to my prospective audience. I've spent most of the last two days bouncing around the net—researching hauntings, UFOs, the unexplained, whatever—and I'm getting nowhere.

When the light goes down and the temperature becomes more bearable, I wander through the souks in the vain hope of finding inspiration. The souks are a labyrinth of cobblestone streets sheltered by high and magnificent stone archways. Many of the streets are like tunnels where you constantly dodge hawkers, donkeys, barrow pushers, vans and African peddlers. There are vegetables, delicacies, quartered animals, fabrics, spices, trinkets and every conceivable type of narjileh. I get lost in the hypnotic, fractal complexity of the patterns on glassware, textiles, copper and silverwork. I sit down at the cafes and play chess with the locals. They defeat me every time.

In an alley leading from the markets, I come across a statue of a Hittite king. He rides a lion and stares into a far-off horizon that must still be there, somewhere. I gaze at his large, almond-shaped eyes and his square, frizzled beard. If he were alive now, I don't think the modern world would seem that strange to him.

In the souk's grimy backstreets, the walls and wooden beams are plastered with the faces of martyrs: children, women, men. They all have names, scores of forgotten names. I even discover posters of bin Laden flapping in the breeze. I wonder who remembers and if it matters. I wonder whether forgetfulness and historical amnesia are not, in the end, the best solution. I guess that, if the story sinks, I can come up with some alternative. Perhaps I can do a piece on neo-pan-Arabic nationalism, or post-war Qiram, or the al-Qaeda Party. Maybe I could interview al-Zhara himself.

My next stop is Jezzir-el-Awr, the last town before the Syrian border. I get the impression that everyone here accepts the reality of the infidel djinn without the slightest surprise or perturbation. It makes perfect sense to them. They already have a place for these things in their cosmology. I'm beginning to grow envious of their certainty, their belief in a universe that is just and meaningful.

Day 11

Jezzir-el-Awr lies on the eastern bank of Nahr Al-Furat, an old farming settlement that suddenly struck it rich when light crude oil was found there in the mid-eighties. Lots of Bedouins and Gezira peasants pass through the town. During the US invasion, the troops promptly took over the installations and claimed the production. They built a refinery so the stuff came out ready to feed the planes and vehicles.

It was the first place that the insurgents reclaimed in the early days of the collapse, and it was a miracle that the whole thing didn't blow up. The Americans built a military base and a whole new suburb, each as large as the old town itself, to house contractors, officials and workers. At one point there were three security personnel per civilian operator, plus a whole infantry division on guard.

The suburb was a surreal vision of small-town, middle-class America in the middle of the desert, still visible below the layers of Middle Eastern kitsch—the arabesque wrought-iron fences, faux Persian gardens, added-on turrets. The massive Hummers waiting on the driveways have stayed the same, minus the oil, of course. After the defeat, the shopping centre was torn down and replaced by an impressive mosque. They kept the car park, a sea of asphalt five degrees hotter than the surrounds. Welcome to al-Zhara's cultural revolution.

My hotel room overlooks a jumble of dusty rooftops. I see the souk in the mid-distance and, further, the levy banks containing the river. Tropical vegetation covers the banks, extending into the empty spaces of the town and beyond. I wonder how long it will be before some primeval Mesopotamian creature crawls from the jungle.

I'm sitting at a cafe by the pedestrian suspension bridge, sipping shay, waiting to immerse myself in the long sunset as soon as I finish typing. For once, I can fool myself that I'm on holiday.

Tomorrow, the oil rig. I'm giving these ghosts one last chance.

Day 12

In the afternoon, I drive to the rig. It looks like the abandoned playground of a giant child, scattered with upturned water tanks, sunken shacks, collapsed fences and drill pipes. Everything is covered with a thick layer of sandy dust. Dark-green creeping vines have pushed through every available interstice. The derricks lean precariously, and the cable spools and hoisting systems dangle from exhausted beams. The mud pumps and control houses are almost completely submerged in weeds and soil. There are four hammer pumps frozen at the peak of their upward thrust, a slightly menacing gesture left forever unfinished. A fifth hammer has collapsed, crushing a row of diesel engines.

Nothing remains of the adjacent military base. Weeds and thickets of long reeds rim the squares and rectangles of dirt where buildings once were. It's been raining for three days now without a break. I stay in the car, watching the motionless structures, waiting for something to happen, for someone or something to appear. The long twilights here remind me of the eerie Australian skies during the Summer of Death, the bushfire season that brought the country to its knees. It's hard to believe that it's been nearly two decades since that happened. That was my last summer in my homeland. Smoke and ash blanketed the sky, shaping the light into otherworldly streaks of pink and white. I haven't thought of this in a while. The desert is doing things to me.

The rain gives me a welcome excuse to stay in the car. I'm not afraid of ghosts but something worse. I'm scared of the void—the possibility that there's nothing out there at all.

Day 14

Well, that was the last chance. I'll fly back to Berlin soon.

In the old days, by this stage, I'd have a wastebasket full of unfinished drafts and false starts, furiously crumpled and stuffed into the bin like I was trying to drown some enemy in a bucket of water. Now, instead, I have a virtual folder sitting somewhere on a remote server, containing all the shameful back-ups that one day I'll have the courage to delete.

Call me old-fashioned, but I miss the days when things were things. The feeling is the same, though: the depressing emptiness of a story going nowhere. Luckily, I found a nice underground bar, catering mainly to foreigners, where the alcohol laws are relaxed or overlooked altogether. I've been drinking a lot, striking up conversations with young travellers.

In the mornings I watch interminable Egyptian soap operas in the hotel's common room, drinking Turkish coffee and watching the procession of Israelis, Czechs, Canadians, North Africans, Indians, Chinese and Americans from both south and north. They are a new breed of tourist, disillusioned and impoverished. Many strike me as withdrawn and aimless. Yet most seem at peace. It comes from having no expectations, I guess.

Tonight, the bar. It's quiet and there are around twenty people, mostly backpackers. The dull rain is audible below the Arab electronica playing over the speakers. The place is set up like a Turkish cafe, with cushions and burning lamps on the tables spreading a dim and cosy light. It's pure kitsch fantasy, but comforting. I'm sitting in one of the booths at the back of the place, propped on cushions, my tablet abandoned on the table.

I'm beginning to doze off when I hear the voice. 'I'll stay for as long as I like, buddy!' The sound is booming yet distant, as though it's coming from the other side of a wall. I'm startled by the accent, a thick southern US drawl I haven't heard in many years. It hits me before I can even decipher the words.

At the service area, a bulky shape totters drunkenly from the bar. As far as I can make out, the man is carrying a large backpack and equipment of some kind. The two guys behind the bar stare with hostility at the newcomer. A palpable sense of fear takes hold of the place. Two young, tanned girls, probably from Northern Europe, are retreating cautiously.

I can just make him out in the dim light. Cropped hair, pasty white skin, tight tank top, round Lennon-style dark glasses. He's tall and muscled in a gym-junkie kind of way, but he looks haggard and underfed. His flesh is colourless, as though his body is feeding off its own muscle. I can't make out what he's carrying, but I know. Suddenly, I know.

I try to disappear into the cushions and make myself inconspicuous, but then the man turns and scans the back wall where the booths are. I notice something different, a subliminal change. It takes me a full minute to realise the rain has stopped. The doors of the bar are open, flapping to the beat of a sandstorm that has wakened, suddenly and inexplicably. The electronica is not enough to dispel the silence.

I'm afraid, almost in shock. My blood has stopped in its tracks. I realise too late that I've been staring at him for some time. He's spotted me and I'm the only one left in the booths. I look away, but I can feel his eyes on me.

I press my fingers around the glass, trying to evoke some response from my numb limbs. As he approaches, I make out camouflage pants and a torn backpack. An assault rifle with a telescopic sight dangles by his side, pointing to the floor. He drags it as though he has forgotten about it. The silver tags twinkle in the light. I see scars, a peeling face, tall army boots caked in sand.

'Hey buddy, you don't mind if I sit here, do ya?' The guy falls on the seat opposite mine. His body makes no sound. His dirty glasses mirror the orange light from the lamps, and his eyes are visible in glimpses, dark and shifting, of an indeterminate colour. I avoid looking into them.

It's hot in here. He should smell of stale sweat and bad breath, but I pick up only a vague scent, like some meat has gone off in a distant kitchen.

'Can I taste your drink? What is it? Looks like a lady's drink.' He casts a glance behind him. 'They won't serve me over there.' His voice seems to come from another direction, somewhere behind him, to his left. I stare at my glass. 'Come on buddy, they're refusing me a drink, they always do around here. Ungrateful vermin.'

He slaps something down on the table. 'Come on, my round.' I haven't seen Washington's face for so long, the memories are almost overwhelming. 'Just go to the bar.' He reaches for my half-empty glass of vodka and cranberry. I retreat instinctively, but, as his blunt fingers are about to touch the glass, he withdraws them with a pained expression. 'Are you always this quiet?'

'You took me by surprise. I… I didn't know you were operating in the area.' My voice sounds thin and constrained.

He cocks his head to the left and smiles, showing a row of straight, white teeth. 'That's better. Much better. Lemme introduce myself. The name's George Francis Johnson. Corporal Johnson, 3rd Division Infantry, Marine Corps, United States Army.'

I say my own name in a wheezing whisper. I can't believe what I'm doing.

He nods. 'Sure.' As he moves his head, I see glimpses of dull light from underneath the glasses. The glasses aren't tinted. They only seem dark because of what's happening beneath them.

My inner journalist takes over. *He can't hurt me. He can't hurt me.* 'You must miss home, Corporal. Whereabouts in the States are you from?'

'Georgia,' he responds immediately. He pauses, gauging my reaction. 'Long way away, yes.'

'Oh, I've been to Georgia. Nice part of the world.'

He seems to relax and sinks into his chair. Without prompting, he tells me about his childhood and family. He has two sisters, both nurses now, and his father was in real estate. The Global Financial Crisis screwed him.

As his words drift in the air, I realise he's talking to himself, clinging to fading memories. With each word, he seems more real. And when silence comes, he drifts away once more. Could it be that he doesn't know what's happening? Time is ticking by, and my inner journalist is debating himself. This is the opportunity of a lifetime, yes, but who will believe me?

'Corporal, why are you here? I mean, fighting this war?' It's a risky question, likely to bring up conflicting emotions. I can sense his rage, but I get the impression he's asked himself the same thing countless times. I glance into his eyes, but the lenses of his glasses are now smooth obsidian.

His answer is mechanical, a rehearsed speech. 'We're fighting this war against the enemies of freedom, those who hate the United States and want to kill and rob us of our freedom.'

'And why do they hate you, Corporal? Why do you think people hate the United States?'

I regret the question the moment it leaves my lips. I sound sceptical of his motives, but he takes it well and thinks about it. 'Because they… they have to hate somebody, and America is the most powerful, richest country in the world. And they look around for someone to blame and say, "Well, let's get *them*." I guess.'

I nod politely, like a therapist. I want to be out of here. There's a sudden pain in my chest, I know it too well, but I must keep talking. I must keep him focused.

'It's been a long, bad war out here, Corporal. When are you going home? Do you know? You must miss your family.'

'Soon.'

A breath of air caresses my face—the smell of hot sand, desert, petrol. When he sticks his hand into his pockets, I give a little jump. He pulls out a piece of paper and places it gently on the table, halfway between us. I lean across. It's a blurry photograph of a young, smiling girl sporting two blonde ponytails and a red dress too large for her. She must be five years old.

'Sally's her name. Haven't seen her...' He frowns. 'In some years, I guess. She's in third grade now.'

Beyond him, the place is empty. The two barmen stand in their place, their shadows watching us.

'Did your wife send you this?'

He hasn't heard me. 'The desert's a hard-arsed bitch, but we will win this war. Like we've won all the other wars.' He shuffles in his chair and looks around, disoriented. He seems to have lost all interest in me. 'It might take longer than anticipated,' he says to the door.

I nod in silence and stare at my empty glass. My eyes are filling with tears. *It's the sand*, I tell myself. *The sand.*

'Good luck, soldier.'

When I open my eyes, he's gone.

Outside, it has begun to rain again. On the table, there's a thin rectangle of dust where the photograph has been. On the seat, a few handfuls of sand trickle onto the floor like the filling from a broken hourglass.

THE SHADOWS AND THE SWARM

It comes with no warning, shadowing the earth like the wings of a predatory bird, at the limbo hour between darkness and dawn when the swarm lapses into a long moment of insect-sleep.

Workers, warriors, children, larvae—the newborn light reveals the bodies of hundreds strewn across the fields, squashed into mounds of black pulp where shattered limbs and occasional fragments of antennae can be seen. Of the once-proud wings of glowing greens and erotic yellows only a pale powder remains, like pulverised diamonds on the soil.

The remaining members confer busily, filling the air with erratic circles and the pained melody of wings. The sight of death is not a novelty. Often, as the swarm carries on its everyday business, they will notice that someone is flying low or lingering too long on a leaf or patch of shade. Next moment, they see their mate swept away by the currents, following its helpless spiral descent, the limbs twitching in robotic farewell. By the time they reach the body, the multifaceted eyes are silent and empty, nothing staring at nothing. The body remains intact and whole, just as in life. A distressing sight, the swarm thinks, as the body is quickly dismembered and transformed into nourishment. Although death claims a heap of them at a time, this is a minor gasp in the collective consciousness, soon forgotten in the tireless movement of the swarm.

Contemplating the devastation, sensing with hair-thin limbs the sticky signature of death in the air, the survivors realise that this is different. Nearly three-quarters of the group have been extinguished in one vast and surreptitious sweep. These are not the cryptic and gradual ways of nature.

What are we to do.
Now?
We can escape
(fear)
We cannot escape
We are safe.
Here.
We have been safe here.
For as long as we.
Can remember.
We must then.
Seek help.
(excitement)
Outside help.

There is a pause in which the scattered voices gather into one thought, reaching a decision.

We will alert.
The authorities.
The Office.

The swarm huddles together, suspended, beating in synchrony. Although they have little hope in the insect bureaucracy, it seems the only ones they can resort to.

The task of lodging a report to the Office is allocated to one of the older members, an insect named White on account of its albino colour. The emissary rides the currents, outwards into the fields surrounding the nests, then into the reaches beyond. As the day turns into night, White spots a rim of soil marked with faint but recognisable molecules of smell. It is an entrance into an underground maze.

The moist enclosure of the tunnels welcomes White as it follows one of the paths into the heart of the Office. As it advances, the air becomes humid and the concoction of smells sweeter and overpowering. It occasionally comes across a public servant on its way out or a group of peasants chattering among themselves, seemingly lost in the tunnels. Eventually, it arrives at a chamber illuminated by a dull luminescence from no apparent source. At the centre of the chamber there is a reception desk, attended by a large praying mantis of unwavering eyes.

As it waits for its turn, White inspects the variety of species in the room, some of which it has never seen before. There is a thin mosquito with emerald wings and a large sting which it carries with visible pride. There is a silver bug with many eyes studying hostilely the surroundings while abstractedly weaving a cocoon of faintly shining threads. There are schools of baby flies moving in feverish patterns. There is a fat translucent worm picking nervously on the dirt and regurgitating clumps of it.

Some of the visitors are here to register unusual events or notify the higher authorities of migrations, Shadow movements and areas of benign weather. Others bring offerings to the mythical Tetzoacal, the Queen of the Office, or carry curious things to be stored in the Library. Others are here to settle disputes or to find jobs.

All are welcome. All are equal before the Office.

They are called one by one and directed into different passages. The conferences are brief and conducted in low tones. When its turn comes, the emissary glides before the desk and is asked to state the reason for its visit.

A great catastrophe has befallen us, the old insect explains. *Hundreds have died inexplicably.*

White fashions a mental representation, trying to encapsulate the horror of what has happened. Despite the intensity of its thought, the receptionist's expression does not betray any interest or emotion.

No signs of Shadows?

I beg your pardon?

No sudden darkness? Sodden smell obscuring the air? Abrupt abyss in the sky?

No. One moment they were, the next they weren't.

Hmmm. It is a rather curious account. You will have to speak to the General Secretary.

An antenna points towards the mouth of one of the passages. The emissary emits a thanks and proceeds.

The Secretary's chamber is cosier and more pleasant than the reception area. Two globes of chemical light glow in the far corners. The Secretary is an old bug who is missing its rear legs. The remaining ones fidget constantly over a messy stack of papers.

Hello, the bureaucrat says, speaking rapidly. *What can I do for you?*

We emerged from sleep this morning to find most of our swarm killed in a most gruesome manner.

White sends another mental image, but this time it comes out faded and sketchy. The outrage is distant now, replaced by growing awe at the ancient ways of the Office.

I see, says the Secretary. *I believe there have been similar occurrences throughout history, vast and seemingly absurd acts of… erm… Shadow intervention.*

The emissary's wings flutter with excitation. *You mean, there is an explanation?*

The Secretary looks up from its papers and examines its interlocutor for a long moment. Unreadable thoughts flicker across the cells of its eyes.

Things are not that simple, it chirps dryly. Sensing the visitor's agitation, the bureaucrat rises a placating limb and laboriously shifts position behind the desk.

Let me explain. I foresee, in this case, four distinct possibilities.

The first possibility is that, indeed, there is an explanation for what has happened, an answer within the reaches of our understanding. If this is the case, it means that a routine investigation shall clear the matter to your satisfaction and determine the cause of so much senseless death.

The second option is the diametrical opposite of the first. We shall never understand what has happened, since we have no insight beyond our insect condition. An explanation may exist at a higher level of understanding, but this explanation would seem to us absurd, unintelligible or maybe perhaps too cruel and terrifying. So our attitude must be one of resignation and humble reverence towards the greater forces which control our existence. Or maybe we can choose a stand of defiance and permanent revolt as a way of expressing some kind of individual or collective self-affirmation.

The General Secretary taps its limbs on the table. *Are you following me?* Dangling atop the thin stem of its neck, White's head nods vigorously.

Third possibility. There is no explanation whatsoever, either within or beyond our understanding or any kind of understanding. In which case, no course of action or thought would be more legitimate than any other.

Fourth option. We can fashion an explanation ourselves and all agree to uphold it. Regardless of its mythical or fictional character, this explanation might serve to dispel our terror and make our lives happier—insofar as we teach our progeny to preserve it throughout the generations, uphold it as an unchanging truth and not to question it too closely.

The Secretary stares at the blank expression of the visitor. The speech has finished, but a long time passes before the old emissary realises this.

Well? the bureaucrat says finally.

Oh. The words have only filled White with unease. *So, is there an explanation or not?*

The Secretary rubs its proboscis in consternation, rummages through a pile of papers and takes a fresh form. *I will send an Investigator to take a look. Routine procedure. Then, we'll see what we can do. Please take this and proceed to the waiting room.*

The waiting room is smaller and less well-illuminated than the Secretary's chamber. The emissary fills out the form, marking the multiple-choice squares with chemical traces. Then it curls into a ball and rests on the earth, listening to the soothing murmurs of the ground. After a while of waiting, a voice comes from the doorway and breaks the reverie.

Good morning. My name is Tzzt, Office Investigator.

The accent is muddy and slow. White realises that the Investigator is too large to fit into the room. They meet at the doorway, and their antennas exchange friendly signals.

Tzzt leads the way through the tunnels and back towards the surface. The Investigator is a golden female blowfly of faded wings and a mean-looking sting, a talkative yet distant kind of creature.

As they cruise through the insect maze, the Investigator questions the emissary about the swarm, about their way of life, their beliefs and social organisation. From White's responses, Tzzt can gather that they are a classless and harmonious society, yet superstitious, territorial and set in their ways.

After so many tunnels, the emissary finds itself yearning for the warmth of daylight and the embrace of the swarm.

The insects welcome the Investigator with a certain suspicion. Tzzt shows no sign of being offended or even noticing. The sight of the massacre has immediately absorbed her attention. The motionless eyes examine the scene, the forest of gnarled bodies in the cold light. Sometimes the universe can be so cruel, so indifferent to the fate of the insect kind. This is one of the worst things

Tzzt has seen over her long life. Could this be the work of the Shadows, those colossal and malignant deities who often delight in such genocide and destruction?

A part of the swarm is busy laying neat piles of excreta in circles around the dead while humming a mournful hymn in remembrance. Another part is hatching in the hope of building their numbers up. They lay circles of sperm under the shade of leaves and fill the wind with the frail electricity of coded calls. Atop the swaying stems of grass, the glistening pearls await the buzzing dance of the carriers.

As the insects work, they cast occasional glances at the new-comer and talk among themselves.

A curious apparition.

From a distant.

Place.

So large and.

Clumsy.

A life so safely removed from the struggle of everyday existence.

Yes.

What can it do?

At best, all the Office can offer is explanations.

And what is the use of explanations now?

Yes.

Can explanations bring our loved ones back?

No!

Presently, following a tacit signal, they gather around Tzzt.

Sensing the distrust lurking across the insect-mind, the Investigator remains suspended in the air, facing the group, studying them one at a time, the same mind staring from dozens of eyes.

First of all, she says, *I would like to convey on behalf of the Office our most sincere and felt condolences.*

The swarm stares with indifference.

I know how it feels to have your loved ones killed like that. I know how it feels to live without explanations.

And thus, Tzzt tells them the story of her life.

Long before I was recruited into the Office, I lived in a large colony in the tropics. I can still evoke the heat, the light and shadow dances of vegetation, the ripe atoms of perception. Over the seasons, our population expanded its dominion for miles, outgrowing all other species in the area. My first memories are of a dark and cold birth-chamber, where I wriggled blindly with a thousand others. The nurses inspected and cleaned me, then taught me about the body and the organisation of understanding. I remember the sheltering warmth of the nests, the first glimpse of the open sky and the streets of our kingdom.

My infancy was happy. I was born a worker, and every day I headed with my fellow labourers into the outskirts, where we toiled tirelessly, annexing ground and expanding the network of nests.

Then the trouble started. As I neared full adulthood, I felt the call of reproduction. It began with a series of strange dreams. Then my body began to swell and overflow with a thick milky liquid. The bureaucrats came to carry away the affected workers, gathering and leading them into the core area of nests, where we worked our way down through ancient systems of passages.

We alighted at the mouth of a round corridor. I remember standing in the queue, breathing in the collective fear and adding my own, as one by one my comrades were summoned into a wide entrance rimmed with stones.

When my turn came, I was directed into a sumptuous room where the Queen waited, spread-legged and glowing with insane desire. I was immediately transfixed by her beauty, the delirious dance of her limbs and eyes like viscous precious stones.

The moment of insemination was brief, yet timeless. I was so much in love I could not drive her out of my mind. The Queen's terrifying beauty can nowadays only be compared to that of Tetzoacal, the Great Bureaucrat Queen, who is said to rule over the workings of the Office. I knew my fellow workers felt the same way and a murderous jealousy arose between us. Warriors kept watch over us night and day.

Meanwhile, time and time again, we were led through the corridors and exposed to the Queen, who became more ferocious at each encounter. She claimed our seed till the last drop, often sinking her mandibles into our bellies to drink the pearly substance.

Rumours began to spread. They said that once the inseminations were finished, we would all be put to death. The days grew long and tense, but we never found out our fate, because, shortly after, the Shadows arrived.

At best, the Shadows had been the stuff of legend and folklore. Sure, we had heard of nearby populations being wiped out, but we never thought it could happen to us. Thus, when the ground began to tremble and the wind changed direction, everyone assumed freak weather was upon them, and they carried on their daily activities as if nothing was the matter.

But then, a peculiar, sickening smell filled the air, so powerful that many were instantly drawn to it and driven mad. Long bubbling insect streams rushed in all directions, some racing towards the Shadows, other scampering over buildings and the writhing bodies of fellow beings.

Then the sky blackened. Suddenly, enormous shapes loomed over our city.

Soon I was too busy trying to keep alive, for the workers had taken advantage of the situation to allow free rein to their murderous impulses.

The earth cried, trembled open. Crowds broke into chaos and pushed at every side. The air burnt with panic as we saw our houses and canals, our streets and corridors, the whole of our glorious kingdom stomped out of existence by the advancing, stinking darkness, destroying in an instant what had taken many lifetimes, hazy ancestral aeons to build.

In the distance, in the dark sea of movement, I saw the Queen climbing out from the ruins, fearful and broken, staring pleadingly at the dark shapes as the sky closed in on the earth. The Queen was not beautiful anymore.

Those of us lucky enough to escape gathered in groups and wandered for many moons and many suns until a contingent of bureaucrats intersected our path. I was offered work in the Office and eventually became an Investigator. After a few months, my body changed again into that of a female, an aborted Queen with a long sting and this shell of gold. In this manner, the advent of the Shadows was a blessing in disguise.

The Investigator climbs up in the air and does a small pirouette, signalling the end of her story. The myriad melancholy facets of her eyes encompass the now enraptured attention of the swarm.

Now listen carefully, she says. *I have a plan.*

And so they go and get themselves a Shadow. Upwards into the rarefied heights of the air, then down in spirals, circumventing the trunks of trees, the uneven terrain, Tzzt leading the way, catching with her claw-like mandibles and tasting in her mouth the densities of space, the fluctuations of light and smell. Trailing the faint Shadow scent.

The swarm-mind glows with fear as they sporadically probe the surroundings with nervous twitches of limbs, not knowing what to look for. Their eyes flicker about, following the outlines of the new landscape.

Onwards through the unfamiliar space. Onwards as the soft morning gives way to the harsh geometries of noon.

There is movement now, newborn quivers and unnatural darkening. The appearance of the Shadow is like a sudden and disorienting blackout. The swarm mind freezes. Its atoms halt in the air, breaking formation, but the Investigator urges them on.

This is one of the things that killed your people, she says, struggling onwards, into the colossal presence. Heavy currents toss them about like dry leaves. The depths of the Shadow are teeming with life. Some members fall prey to the intoxicating atmosphere and drop away into the darkness, their rambling thoughts echoing away into silence.

And there are many more.

Of these...

(horror)

Roaming.

The earth.

The wind casts them into illogical orbits, and in the midst of chaos they see the Investigator plunging straight into the maelstrom of the Shadow, flying backwards, sting-first into It.

It seems like it is the end of the world. The currents of the ether grow more violent still. Their wings beat against the fury to no avail. The sky is a deafening mass. But then, just as suddenly, all disturbance dies down. The air clears, and space settles into customary patterns of smell and dark. Tzzt emerges from the fallen Shadow, a golden beam rising from a vast continent of night.

Come on, she says weakly. *You must learn to live without fear.* Tzzt's sting has gone, leaving a long gash on her back. Two of her legs are twisted and broken, and her flight is unsteady.

Now, the Shadow is all yours.

Hesitation, then ripples of desire, across the insect mind. The swarm descends, curious, hungry, afraid on the defeated Shadow. They land on the open eyes and skate on the moist and glassy surface. They slip into the warm openings of mouth and nostrils and ear canals, crawling under layers of clothes, into caverns and folds and sliced slots of flesh. Bodies play entangled in the long strands of hair.

They dig wounds into which they lay fresh eggs. Others peck at the soft flesh and wash their limbs in lagoons of blood. Others drown and lie dead, belly up, happier to be that way.

As the mind rejoices, it grows dizzy, drunk and forgetful. The Investigator contemplates the spoils, the partial victory, without taking part. As she examines the contours of the Shadow from the heights, she begins to word in her mind the report to be later presented at the Office.

There are still no answers, Your Highness, no explanations, but the people are happy, at least for today. Small victories: it is possible that this is all we can claim.

Debilitated by the loss of her sting, the Investigator looks to land on a dark and cool patch of vegetation she has sensed from the air, but one of her wings fails and does not respond.

She spirals upwards in the air. There is not much time, she knows. She has always hoped it would be different, that she would face this moment calmly and without terror. She remembers the birth-chamber, a vivid flashback of her male soft body packed against the hardening cocoon with timeless gaps of shadow and faint light caressing his eyelids. She sees childhood corridors, faces of old warriors and workers.

The swarm continues the feast, unaware, and she senses her strength ebbing, memory and world merging, an abyss, helpless limbs flickering from her belly.

As she drifts downward, in a dying trajectory towards the ground, Tzzt is overcome by the certainty that she is being observed.

I WILL NEVER LEAVE YOU

Sandra worked in the cubicle six spaces from mine, where before there was a guy named Carlos. The turnover of employees is a routine event in the stale and cyclical universe of the office, and the faces that come and go are shadows that slip by against the background of my life. But with Sandra it was different. Something intense and elusive made her stand out from that first day. She was a girl in her thirties, petite, plump and pale-skinned. I don't remember the colour of her eyes, but they were dark.

Sandra was a beautiful woman in her own way. The few times we spoke, our conversation was cordial and generic. I liked to watch her in secret. I admired her deep black hair that bloomed with a life of its own, like an alien plant. The strict bun could not contain the creature and the curls always escaped, peering at us blindly like the tentacles of the Medusa.

Something distantly sensual murmured at the junction of her neck and jaw. I must clarify that these moments of abstract eroticism only accidentally involved her. Sometimes the outline of a building against a clear sky or the roar of a truck on an avenue stirred in me the same sexual tingle, distant and theoretical. My attraction was something ideal. I fantasised about her playing a role analogous to mine, a survivor in a post-capitalist, post-apocalyptic world, struggling to maintain sanity in the catacombs of corporate bureaucracy. With her austere dress code, Sandra played a character, someone devised as a bastion against the world. There is no better place to hide (I know it well) than before everyone's eyes.

Like me, she lived in hiding and didn't fit in anywhere. Those eyes betrayed her, changing colour with the whims of the light, always sheltering a heart of pure darkness. Her fragile presence evoked in me a sense of absence. Often it was as if Sandra was not there. During our years in the office, I was struck at times by the sudden fear that she had vanished, and it became a habit to turn in my chair to make sure she was still in her cubicle.

True, I could have started with Alberto, but I suppose I didn't because Alberto was already a familiar presence in my life at that time. It would be difficult to reconstruct the origins of our relationship, back when we were attending university, since there hadn't been much of a development. You could say that our relationship reached an early plateau where we had been wandering comfortably ever since.

I should write down these minor details in a separate notebook. It's hard to believe that I'm talking about them in the past. Rather than documenting the events, writing keeps them close, alive in my imagination. I have no doubt that they are in a better world than this.

I got together with Alberto every other Thursday to play chess or go to the movies. Sometimes we added a coffee in the city if our schedules allowed it. We played three games at a time, with even results, although he had a certain advantage over me.

He always wrote down the date and winner of the matches. I never knew why. 'Ours is an eternal championship,' he said. 'The day one of us dies—and I warn you that we're all going to die someday, in case you didn't know—on that day, the winner will be decided.'

We had some mutual friends with whom we hung out from time to time, but the truth is that I didn't know much about Alberto. I'm not sure if this was because there wasn't much to know or because he hid it well. Anyway, to understand our relationship, you must understand me first. We are all common and ordinary, but some of us are more common and ordinary than others.

I live alone in a little apartment that my mother bought me, may she rest in peace. I have not had a romantic relationship with a woman in ten years, neither deep nor superficial. I am somewhat overweight. I mean, I'm fat, maybe very fat. I watch porn on the internet every night. When walking, I try not to step on the lines on the pavement.

In my effort to appear normal, I have erased anything that could define me as an individual. After so many years of taking refuge in myself, trying to preserve from society what I thought made me unique, there is no longer anything of my own to keep. Well, there are some things scattered around, but I don't know if they are useful.

I walk through the markets and fairs of Buenos Aires. I go to San Telmo, Chacarita, the Flea Market. I never buy anything. I like marble statues, especially horses. I like to find hidden shops, little caves where arcane things are sold: collector trains, helmets and medals from the Second World War, comics, pottery, buttons, old furniture. These places are becoming scarce and you have to dig further to find them.

I walk through the bookstores on Corrientes and Rivadavia Avenues. I look for old copies of obscure and extinct works. I scan the books and meticulously return them to their place. I take great pleasure in brushing the layers of dust on the covers and shelves, and in sneezing loudly. I carefully observe faces in the street, on the bus, in the subway. This has gotten me into trouble a few times, but I can't help it.

I like to witness the demolitions of old buildings, then walk by a few months later to see the hideous, anonymous new towers rising. It is a melancholic happiness, indistinguishable from sadness. Now I'm sounding like Alberto.

For these and other reasons, Alberto's company was pleasant to me. Somehow his abstract conversation eased the heaviness of the routine and the ordinary. We had exhausted the subject of our intimate lives shortly after meeting and there wasn't much to tell on my side. What he told me about his life were details: what he ate; bills; things that needed fixing around the house; certain curious statistical correlations he saw at work, such as that between a person's shoe size and their propensity for divorce.

Alberto worked as an accountant in an insurance company. His uncle was the boss. He never told me of any woman. As far as I know, he had been single all his life. Of politics and sport, nothing. He did not like football, but as a child he had learned to pretend that he understood and loved it. He yelled 'goal' in unison with his schoolmates. He would look through his Dad's newspaper in the morning to see the results of the matches and memorise some details (who got a red or yellow card, who had kicked or saved a penalty), and then he discussed it with the other boys. The others never suspected anything, he told me with a smile.

We took turns meeting in his apartment and mine. He lived on the fourteenth floor of a building in Barracas, in a narrow apartment with wide, dusty windows that the sun hit directly in winter. His furniture and belongings didn't reveal much about him. Everything was justified according to utilitarian criteria, including the framed photos of his family: nephews; his uncle and uncle's wife; a sister who lived in New York. A couple of times I ran into his uncle, a nice guy who looked a bit like Alberto.

What both appealed to and bored me about Alberto was his fondness for cheap metaphysics and Martian anthropology. He announced his hackneyed revelations as if he himself were the

Aristotle who had first discovered them. At some point, it occurred to me to start recording his utterances, to write a kind of encyclopaedia of them.

I decided to record the ones I could remember.

'There are two possibilities. Everything in the universe is determined in advance, and everything happens according to a logical necessity—or everything is governed by chance and each moment is unique, unrepeatable and devoid of purpose.'

'Time is a subjective property, a product of the mind that observes it and also produces it.'

'The human being is the only animal that carries its own water and food on its back. He needs an artificial skin because his own is weak. He is truly a defenceless being, an unfinished animal that now, incredibly, reigns over the world.'

'The other day, when I was at the hardware store looking for a specific kind of screw, I had the revelation that everything was interconnected. That screw had to have a corresponding nut and a piece of wood, and that wood a hinge, and then a frame. And all those things fit together perfectly—they need each other—so if you alter one you have to alter everything. And I wondered if all the world is like that, so that if you move one thing, everything collapses.'

If everything is written in the universe, and the apparently haphazard flow of becoming is the mocking mask of an immutable Being, then the only purpose of my life has been to arrange for Sandra and Alberto to meet. I was the catalyst for something vast and more significant than my own existence. I'm grateful that the universe threw at me this crumb of transcendentality in what would otherwise be an inconsequential life.

It amazes me that I can recall that fateful day so clearly since there seemed no reason to retain it in such detail. Everything proceeded very ordinarily, with Alberto and I standing at a corner on Santa Fé Avenue. An infernal heat tortured the city, one of those days commonly held as evidence of global warming. The air was a damp broth that passed through clothing, skin, fat and muscle. It laughed at everyone and settled deep inside the bones.

The power had gone out in my apartment. We went down the three floors in the dark. I carried the chess board. While Alberto finished his cigarette, I went into the cafe to check if it had air conditioning. As I left, I saw Sandra at the stop light on the opposite corner, getting ready to cross the street in our direction. Alberto finished his cigarette and I thought it appropriate to wait there to greet her. She appeared to be dressed in her office clothing, except her hair was down, and she wore a wide-brimmed hat and dark glasses. As she approached, I noticed that she had a light skirt and blouse and that only the colour of the clothes was the same indefinite blue or grey.

She did not seem to sweat or suffer from the heat. She was walking with her head down, but she noticed my presence when crossing the street. I know she was debating whether to say hello or pretend to be lost in thought. Finally, she decided to give me a smile as she passed.

'Hello, Sandra', I said, and I heard Alberto imitating me, or rather parodying me in an almost inaudible gasp. Sandra slowed down and stopped a few steps from us. I'm still not certain what caught her attention. She looked at Alberto and blinked twice behind the glasses, but Alberto wasn't a very attractive guy.

'What are you playing?' she said in a shrill voice.

It occurred to me that Alberto would like to meet her, not her particularly, but any woman, so I shut up and passed the ball to him.

'Chess,' he said, choking on the words.

Sandra did not smile often. When she did, her face changed radically. 'That's good!'

There was an uncomfortable pause. I took a deep breath. The air was boiling. Then, Sandra said, 'I was runner-up in the national tournament once.' It seemed that she was getting ready to leave, her whole posture pointed in the direction opposite to us. She even took a couple of tiny steps. Alberto looked at her, stupefied. He gasped again, more audibly. 'I'll play you.'

The three of us sat at a table in the back. I was waiting for the right moment to leave, but it was very nice in there and the prospect of returning to the darkness of my apartment was depressing. I unfolded the board ceremoniously and placed the pieces without asking, white for her, black for him. Neither moved to help me. They waited for me to finish as if my servitude had been dictated in the natural order of things.

The game, I must admit, was fascinating, full of unexpected moves. Alberto defended himself as best he could, but suffered heavy casualties at first, then got nervous and made a couple of bad plays. The checkmate found Albert's king blocked by his own useless subjects and besieged from two stark angles.

There was a long silence in which Alberto and Sandra contemplated each other. Their coffee had long since grown cold. I even remember that, when the waiter brought the coffee, Alberto picked up the salt shaker by mistake, only realising it at the last moment. I decided it was time to go. I was waiting for someone to speak or start the rematch. They could return the board to me later. Then Alberto dropped one of his philosophical pearls. 'The universe is like a chess tournament that never repeats itself.'

Sandra did not seem to understand and did not pretend to. Hence the conversation flowed unevenly. They insisted that I stay, so I played a game with her. I resisted, but she promptly identified my weak spots and rammed into them. I bled from one thousand wounds. From time to time, I looked at her surreptitiously. I could no longer relate that woman in front of me to the Sandra of the office. I don't know if it was the light, her hairstyle, or her expression of extreme focus, but it was like being with her twin sister, someone the same only different.

The neck and sleeves of her blouse were embroidered with fantasy flowers in a spiral shape, nonsensical details that remain vividly imprinted in my memory. That afternoon we spoke more than we had throughout the three-odd years since her arrival at the company. I didn't learn much about her life. Her tastes seemed common enough. She had a cat, went to the movies with her friends once a week, read fashionable books, liked classical music, tried to stay out of office politics. Only her love of chess marked her as rare or unusual. I sensed more intensely than ever that energy I had picked up the moment I first saw her, the energy she tried to hide under an ordinary appearance.

I left them under the pretext that I needed to check if the power had returned to my apartment. Upon reaching the entrance, I found that everything remained just as dark and sad. I went up the three floors and lay down in the gloom. I had a bad headache and blamed it all on global warming.

The following week, I exchanged a few words with Sandra over lunch. She smiled subtly, as if we shared a secret. I spoke with Alberto briefly over the weekend and we arranged to meet the next Friday. I was certainly curious to know what had happened the rest of that afternoon.

On Friday the two of them showed up at my apartment with wine, ravioli, cheese and sauce. I hid my astonishment the best I could. Alberto and Sandra were two parts of my life that until now had not made contact. Amid the lively conversation, the glasses of wine and the games of chess, I became accustomed with surprising speed to the fact that they were a couple. It was even strange for me to conceive of them otherwise.

Seeing them so happy highlighted my own loneliness and anguish. Perhaps I envied their happiness and resented the way they had turned love, a laborious and complex task, into something so simple and spontaneous. Why so much running around, then? Why the loneliness, the reproaches, the vulnerability, the fear, the isolation? For their part, they did not consider it necessary to give me explanations. She laughed at Alberto's clichéd witticisms and he carefully observed her lips as she spoke. I had never seen Alberto drink alcohol or laugh with his mouth open.

On Sunday, just over a week after ravioli night, Alberto told me that he could only hang out for a while, enough to play one game. I didn't ask him what he had to do, but I figured. I waited for him to broach the subject in his own time and way. His mind was on something else and I beat him without a problem. He didn't even bother to write down the result in his notebook.

'It seems to me that I fell in love. Lost and deeply,' he said.

'Already? In two weeks?'

'With an unprecedented intensity, like never before or after.' Only then did he seem to register what I had said to him. 'What does time have to do with it? Aren't new things as true or real as the old ones?'

'Love is fast and sharp.'

He ignored my sarcasm. I regretted being so bitter and a spoilsport. When he was about to leave, he thanked me for introducing him to Sandra. I shrugged. Really, I hadn't done anything. It was amazing that these two creatures, socially incompetent, extraordinary in their ordinariness, had hit it off so well. I imagined them talking, having ice cream, making love, but it was hard for me to conceive of Sandra in anything other than that indefinite colour she wore everywhere. It didn't bother me so much that I envied them as that I didn't know why. I would like to fall in love, who wouldn't? I think I loved two or three women in my life, a long time ago. I remember their names, irrelevant now. Their faces are indefinite blurs.

I began to secretly long for the end of their relationship. The fullness of their lives only put into relief the loneliness of mine. How long could it last? From then on, the meetings with Alberto became shorter but more frequent. Once a week we would see each other on our own and play the usual three games or go to the movies. After a couple of hours, I noticed he'd become restless and his eyes were flitting from side to side. Once, when I was taking my time to say goodbye, he began to sweat like a drug addict anticipating his dose.

At the office, Sandra and I talked more often, and sometimes we had lunch together. She was much friendlier and more open with me. From time to time her gaze became absent and she touched her cheeks dreamily with the tips of her fingers, as if trying to revive the contact of someone or something. She looked prettier, but we could cite the commonplace adage that this always happens to women when they fall in love. I no longer felt the impulse to turn in my chair to see if she was still there, and this indicated two possibilities: Sandra was now here, substantially present, or she was definitely gone so that her absence was now permanent.

Sandra was changing, mutating before my eyes, but very slowly so that it was not noticeable. I suppose the same thing happens to a father who watches his children grow day by day. Sometimes the two of them would come to play chess on a Sunday afternoon and they would bring a bottle of wine and something for dinner. Or I would go to Alberto's and find Sandra there. I noticed changes in his apartment, feminine touches: an air freshener in the bathroom; embroidered tablecloths on the tables. I wondered if Sandra had moved in with him.

The routine and the passage of time managed to bury my adverse feelings. Things went back to normal, except this time normality had a new, indescribable quality, something I can only describe as too normal but that somehow shouldn't be.

When Alberto began to loosen up and talk about his relationship with Sandra, his comments struck me as an extension of his cheap philosophy, now expressed in the form of cheesy love theory.

'I know that love is a subject in which it is easy to get bogged down in the commonplace. The speech of lovers is finite and love, famously, is infinite. Even the mere attempt to express its inexpressibility, as I have just done, leads us to the dead end of platitude. How vulgar is love, how predictable! A place so full of pink sunsets, lazy and sweaty mornings, burning stares, damp and twisted sheets, restless and ecstatic bodies. Of ordinary words transfigured into carnal poetry when whispered softly in the ear. Metaphors worn and eternal, spasms that throw language against its own confines.

'When lovers agree to be silent, because words cannot enclose the deepness and immensity of feeling, they fall into another commonplace, another cliché. Because it is not enough to simply be content with holding the hand of the beloved, one must traverse the skin with the fingertips, renewing the contact as if each touch were the first and could be the last. And each minute of absence bears desperate eternities of yearning for the presence of the loved one, the other who is ultimately oneself.'

When he was with Sandra, he was quiet and at peace. I read the sparkles in his eyes as tears of happiness. He could happily die by her side with a smile. They talked a bit about everything but mostly they preferred to stay quiet. The silences, in fact, grew longer. They could spend the entire afternoon without a word and stay like that, tangled in each other's arms, for hours and hours.

'When we look into each other's eyes, time stops. We immerse ourselves in the other and lose ourselves in the depths, in a being that is now an indistinguishable mixture of two beings. The hours disappear, we fall into a trance, and suddenly we discover each other in the middle of the night, unaware of what has happened.

'Last Monday, for example, we fell into one of those states and we were barely able to get out of the apartment in time for work. We don't even shower and sometimes we forget to eat. It's amazing, but every time I see her, I feel like I haven't seen her in years. Even if she leaves for five minutes, when I come back, I see her with fresh, longing eyes, and I pounce on her, hungry as a wolf. Not only is she the most beautiful woman I have seen in my life, she is the most beautiful thing. She is beauty itself.

'When I look at her, it makes me want to cry, such is the intensity of her beauty. I don't get tired of seeing her, I don't get tired of touching or hugging her. I sincerely believe that at some point the two of us were part of a single organism, a single living being. Perhaps all human beings have been at some point and, due to a cosmic misfortune, have been fragmented into little pieces. I treasure in her absence the crystalline sound of her laugh, the light in her eyes, the brush of her dark hair between my fingers. How sad the world is, Agustín. How sad it is to know that we can all be happy, complete! Being happy is something so simple and within everyone's reach.'

In the last months, the meetings with Alberto became more spaced, and I lost touch with him. When I saw him, he was just as excited and happy, and he talked a lot about Sandra. When we played chess, I nearly always beat them. When Alberto was checkmated, he would blink, as if he'd just awakened, and then he would smile and congratulate me.

A total of eighteen months elapsed between their first meeting and their disappearance. I noticed the first changes in the final two or three months. Sandra started to wear a scarf around her neck. It was the same colour as the rest of her uniform, indescribable, simultaneously grey, navy blue and black depending on the angle of light. She was late and sometimes didn't show up. She didn't deliver things on time and made a lot of mistakes. Our bosses warned her that things couldn't go on like this.

I noticed the marks first on Alberto. They could be seen peering out of his shirt and sleeves, on his neck and forearms. That's when I realised that, since he had started his courtship with Sandra, he'd worn long sleeves. They were the same marks on the skin that Sandra hid with her scarf. From what I could infer from careful glances, the marks were due to some kind of discolouration, the product of dryness or some fungus. It didn't seem proper to ask, and I tried to forget about it.

Not that something was wrong. It didn't feel that way. Maybe everything went very well and is still fine. If it was a tragic or happy ending, it is not for me to decide. The two became distant, and they seemed to lose all interest, not just in me, but in their tasks and responsibilities. And I, for my part, no longer paid much attention to them. I had returned to my loneliness, to my melancholy. It is a comfortable place, the only one I will know, and I cannot complain. I had already resigned myself to the fact that Alberto had abandoned me for a woman. I would no longer find consolation in his childish abstractions.

It was a Thursday. I was invited to dinner at Alberto's. Sandra hadn't been to the office all week. The rumour was that she had fallen sick. Or perhaps the mischievous lovers had fallen asleep in the diffuse light of early spring. Four days in a row! The idea amused me, but it was plausible. I rang the bell and waited at the entrance. I had brought the board and a bottle of wine. I waited a while, rang the bell again, then opened the door. I called their names. The air inside was thick and cushioned the sound. There was a stale and sweet smell, with a hint of burning. It was an animal smell, not entirely unpleasant.

As I moved through the living room, the sound of the pieces inside the box startled me. I felt like I was meddling in something I shouldn't. There was an empty wine bottle on the floor and two plates of unfinished noodles on the table. I stared at the food scraps like an idiot, trying to calculate how long they had been there. The smell was gone, or I was already used to it. I called them again, first Alberto then Sandra. My voice sounded shrill, as if I were screaming.

The sound was like a rubbing—dry and prolonged. It came from the room. I called their names again. I thought of an excuse in case I found them in a compromising situation. They should have listened to me, anyway. As I moved down the hall, I disturbed a couple of flies. I shook them off with my hands.

The window in Alberto's room was wide open. The spring sky outside was cloudy, and the light was flat and even. I stood there on the threshold of the room for a long time while my eyes tried to decipher what they saw. It even took me a few seconds to realise that what I was seeing was not normal, that I shouldn't be seeing this, that no one should ever see it.

Part of them was covered by a dirty sheet, which had once been white. I'm not sure which part it was, I suppose the bottom, because I think I saw some mouths, something like orifices that opened and whispered mutely. There was also something there that had been eyes but that now contemplated themselves, inward, forever in the depth of the other, the loved one. The rash had spread over the entire surface of the skin. In fact, it had taken the place of skin. I can only describe it as exposed flesh. Vulnerable flesh, immensely fragile, reacting with the air, with the brush against itself, poisoned by any impurity.

I don't know if they noticed my presence or if my very presence was what was poisoning them. I don't know whether their movements originated in pain or in a supreme enjoyment now indistinguishable from agony. One limb, in which I distinguished twisted and abnormally arranged fingers—like two sets of opposing forceps—tried to detach itself from the torsos, the central knots where I could make out two dorsal spines playfully entangled like mating snakes. The fingers trying to caress the body. The movement was extremely delicate.

Finally, the tips brushed the surface of the bodies and the flesh shuddered. The echo of that caress traced an indentation in the flesh that was transmitted along the body like a wave until it disappeared under the sheets. I decided then that I should leave them alone. That was my goodbye gesture. I knew that I would not see them again and that I was to leave the board for them on the threshold.

And that was it. I know that at some point the neighbours called the police because of the smell. Traces of blood were found but no other sign of them. I have already told the authorities everything I know, except, of course, the ending. I just told them that I had come in to leave the chess board for them.

Everyone has already drawn their conclusions: macabre sexual games, unpayable debts, depression, suicide pact. The board was never found. That's how I know they are somewhere, that they left together.

I no longer envy them or harbour any grudges. It's strange, but now their joy is part of me. My loneliness feels less overwhelming knowing they're there. In the good days, it's enough to erase the misery of witnessing a happiness denied me.

THE LIFE NEXT DOOR

It begins with that familiar itch, the reflex triggered by a face that resists the tug of remembrance. The incredibly beautiful woman waits on York Street. She stands on the opposite sidewalk, among the peak-hour swarm of corporate slaves, framed by the mannequins in the windows of the Queen Victoria Building. Tom is certain that he recognises her. From somewhere.

Her image flickers between the shadows of buses dashing back and forth. He catches her in a series of glimpses, a fragmented dream. Her sad gaze is lost towards the Town Hall, where the street dies. She does not seem to register the buses that alight at her stop. She is at least thirty, and her hair is dark, reddish and familiar (was it a different hairstyle back then?). She stands impervious to the weary glances and glutinous shifting of office workers, although sometimes her gaze veers, revealing a suppressed anxiety.

Tom strives to remember. A friend of Joanna's? That's the logical explanation. But their relationship is more profound than a mere acquaintance—he knows her very well. It is suddenly imperative not to lose sight of her, if only he could remember why.

At some point, the nagging sensation loses its ordinary character. The intimate familiarity of her presence awakens a sense of strangeness, maybe terror, more powerful and disconcerting than *déjà vu*. Her faltering picture is the only real thing in the tumult. Tom has delved into those eyes for endless hours, in the first light of many dawns, under the last rays of countless dying days.

At 6:26, his bus arrives. Route number 373. It's nearly full. He perceives it from a distance, but he cannot enter it. He cannot be away from her. The bus stops, obstructing his vision. He watches the line of commuters climb up.

When the bus leaves, she is not there. Tom stares at the empty space.

For the rest of the week, he looks for her. He leaves the office at 5:26, 5:31, 6:10, later, but she isn't there.

'Why are you never home on time?' Joanna leans over the kitchen table. A network of fine purple veins runs up her outstretched arms. He hasn't thought of an excuse. His gaze shifts away and inwards, a now-common defence mechanism. He scans the kitchen, noticing the things Joanna has bought for the home: a pink tablecloth, an incense holder, a dozen wine glasses. It's her therapy. She goes shopping and does yoga while he drinks.

The mundanity of the scene awakens a visceral disgust, the last light of dusk pounding against the half-closed shutters, her unwashed hair smeared with coconut oil, the newspaper on the table—why buy it if she never reads it? Little by little she has erased Tom's things, all his traces. One by one, she has taken possession of all the spaces and corners of the house.

'Why do you insist on working overtime?' She looks at him sadly. 'You didn't warn me.'

At the corner of his eye, her gaze pierces him. Her tone could be accusatory, angry or just plain indifferent. Everything in their lives is so ambiguous, shadowy, insincere.

'We're installing a new system,' he says without conviction.

Joanna decides to wash the pots from the night before. She dips her gloved hands in the sink. For a long while he hears the water running, the clanging of pots, the scrubbing of the sponge. The sounds cease and the silence below rises to the surface. Suburban silence, birds chanting messages, a car passing by. He recognises that nervous, dismissive smile.

'I don't give a damn if you're having an affair. I'm just curious.'

'An affair? Where? On the bus?'

The distance suits them well. She paints and has her circle of friends. Twelve years of marriage. They may part ways when they finish paying for the house, but not before.

Luckily, he has one of those jobs that you forget as soon as you clock off. He pays no attention to office politics, customer calls, routine system schedules. The weekend comes and goes like a sigh, and then on Tuesday he sees her, in the same place on the sidewalk, in front of the mannequins.

She is smoking a cigarette. Her long, thin fingers awaken the memories. She smokes twelve a day, sometimes up to fifteen if she has wine. Always white wine, except with pasta and meat. He makes a note of the time: 6:24. He last saw her two Tuesdays ago. Finally, he has unveiled a regularity of sorts.

His bus arrives at 6:26, and he can't stop looking at her. The flow of memories intensifies—memories that are not, *cannot be*, his. A place on the beach. What was it called? A one-story house, a rusty iron fence. Peeling green paint, cracking between his fingers.

The bus pulls away and she is gone. He registers the number: 787. He already knows that number, of course. For a disconcerting moment, the memories flash vividly, dwarfing the busy growl of central Sydney.

There is a girl, five years old, in blue cloth pyjamas, her knees dirty, her hair golden and long. The crowds fall silent, and the coming and going of vehicles is absurd and nauseating. The girl smiles, and he feels like he is falling.

His bus arrives and he finds a spot inside. He feels he has left himself behind at the stop, or perhaps gone with her on the other bus. What remains is a body, a residue each time more remote from his soul.

Maybe it's all a strange sexual fantasy. It wouldn't surprise him. Tom and Joanna's sexual life is agonising, a reflection of their affective life, a reflection of everything. They might do it six times a year and only when very drunk. Or perhaps it's a harbinger of the entropy of middle age. That wouldn't surprise him either. Will the famed middle age be like this, so desperate and sad? Will he scheme elaborate fantasies with any woman that passes by?

Perhaps he has seen her fleetingly at some place, on the street or at a previous job. Maybe he noticed her beauty and his unconscious built a hypothetical reality around her. Can he really be that unhappy? That crazy?

On Friday, after leaving the office, Tom heads to the underground parking lot in the corporate tower. It smells of damp confinement, stale air, car oil, urine. The identical levels are identified by colours, letters and numbers on concrete columns. Where has he parked the car? He looks for the keys in his pockets. Surely, he can unlock his car from a distance and locate it by the beep. As he does every afternoon. But he can't find the keys.

Purple A9. Orange B10, B22… Go down another level. Green C32, C33… Expensive cars, executive cars. His car can't be here. He struggles to remember what colour it is, where he parked it. On the yellow level, he realises his mistake. He doesn't have a car. He takes the bus every day to and from home. Samantha thinks that it's… Is that her name? No, it's Joanna. *Joanna.*

He rotates on his ankles and heads outside. The place has become overwhelming, the low ceilings, the beams and columns, the windowless walls. Everything looms and recedes at the same time. There's no air, he can't breathe. He looks for the EXIT signs. Joanna owns a car, a red Mazda that he never drives. He did have a Nissan Pintara... back in 2006...

He's sweating torrentially but can't decide if he's hot or cold. He pushes the exit door open and ascends the concrete stairs. He feels heavy, his strength draining. The stairwell is even narrower and more stifling, an *animal* odour. He imagines that the ramps and levels continue infinitely in all directions, down to the heart of the earth and towards the heavens. He will never get out of there.

On one of the landings, Tom detects a sliver of light coming from a crack below a door. He pushes and emerges into the daylight. The distant scent of the ocean greets him, a limpid and ephemeral gust of salt, waves and foam garlands. The sunlight floods his eyes, the street, the world. He rips off his jacket like a piece of old skin and a few coins fall from his pockets onto the sidewalk. The coins tinkle, give off sparks and roll into the gutter.

Gradually, he catches his breath. He wipes the sweat from his forehead with the cuff of his shirt and looks at the grimy stain on the light-blue fabric. He reminds himself of his name, his age, his wife's name, the bus he takes every day. The familiar world falls into place, reluctantly, as though it doesn't want to be here.

Peak hour. The smell of junk food, coffee, rancid perspiration, smog. Here comes the 373, and a window seat, a humble victory.

It might be Tuesday. He's no longer interested in what day it is. He sees her again, for the fourth time. As soon as she takes her predetermined spot and assumes her defensive pose, Tom heads for the cross walk. He doesn't know what he's doing, he doesn't want to know. Perhaps he is confused. Maybe it's all a mistake, but he must end this madness once and for all.

He goes out into the patio with his daughter in his arms. A brick path winds through beds of flowers and herbs. On the last promontory of grass at the edge of the beach, there's the white plastic table with matching chairs. He has seen the chairs fly off when the wind is rough, and he's had to fetch them from the sand a few times.

As he approaches, their eyes lock. She doesn't recognise him, and her poise hardens. Tom wants to hug her. He turns to one side to avoid heading straight into her. He knows *exactly* how it feels to kiss her long neck. He knows the warm electricity in his hands as they meander through the hollows and curves of her body.

You missed her first steps today! You should have seen her... Red suits you...

Tom is aware of his ragged appearance. He doesn't sleep well, and he's lost his appetite. He fights with Joanna every night, and all he sees in the mirror in the morning is a blur.

The ocean has many faces. It's amazing the amount of clothes a kid goes through in one day!

'Excuse me.' She shivers, yanked from her lethargy. Her surprise turns to alertness, then a hint of fear before settling into the standard blankness. It's *her*, no doubt. Her eyes look at him with that studied distance he recalls to perfection. Her scent, floral and sharp and cheap, makes him think of sand.

She looks different. A tad skinnier. Tired, maybe. She stands tense and on the defensive.

'Yes?' Her voice is just as he remembers it.

'I think I know you from somewhere.' This is all going wrong. It's the oldest phrase in the pick-up manual for desperate perverts. *Do you come here often?* Samantha's brow twitches and three perfect lines appear on her forehead. 'It's just that... well. Sorry. My name is Thomas... Tom...'

The woman's eyelids narrow. She's staring at him with open hostility. She's going. He's losing her. *Dad, when is Mum coming back?*

Samantha. How many times has he cried, muttered, laughed, sighed that name? The attention of the office drones gathers around them. He can feel them closing in. He can see himself through their eyes: the kind of scoundrel who tries to chat up girls at bus stops. Her lips twist. Pain... Tom thinks he understands what's happening. However, what he thinks is happening is impossible.

'Tom,' she says to herself. What flashes in her eyes is recognition, but not the kind he was after.

He's storing the mower in the shed. The intoxicating smell of freshly cut grass. The clouds—it's going to rain. A voice behind him, a child's little voice.

'What kind of sick joke...' She doesn't finish the question. Her tears bubble up, quickly flooding her eyes and running down her cheeks.

The girl is watching television. Colours flutter across the screen. She's dressed stylishly, with a bow on her clean and shiny hair, about to go to the birthday party of a friend. In her gaze, there is an infinite capacity for wonder.

Tom senses—more than sees—the shadows approaching and crowding around. Voices, men. *Hey you! Leave her alone.* Tom turns back and walks blindly down the pavement, away from her. *Are you okay, miss?* He tries to rip his body from the aura of her presence, leaning his weight to one side, looking for the crosswalk. He stumbles at the curb, manages to keep his balance, and throws himself across the street without looking.

A bus rushes past and Tom hastens his steps. All around, the diffuse shadows convene. Indecipherable shapes, faces merging into each other. It's amazing that he has managed to cross without getting killed, but he is safe on the other side now. Alive, at least, where he started. Squealing masses of vehicles hide him from the eyes on the other side of the street. There's fleeting relief. He turns towards the Town Hall and walks aimlessly, away from there. It seems to him that everyone is watching him accusingly at the periphery of his vision. His feet seem to slip in the same place as in a dream.

It's hard to leave her like this, so heartbroken. With great effort, he fights the urge to look back at her. He can't go home. The mere prospect of seeing Joanna depresses him. The prospect of lying again, lying all the time. He's a ghost, floating above the street, the dark river of the city seeping around him. His feet hammer on the street. The feeling of being observed is excruciating. Observed by no one in particular, maybe by the city itself.

He reaches Liverpool Street and turns right without thinking. He catches sight of a sign: THE SPANISH CLUB. Here he will be safe, even for a little while. Darkness has descended, but he hasn't noticed. Shadows crawl from their hiding place. He signs the guest book and sits in a corner, as sheltered as possible, under the TV tuned to a loud game show in Spanish.

He observes the characters of the place. No one seems to suspect anything. Tom thinks he can see other faces stirring darkly, spectral beings that imitate the movements, gestures and expressions of their hosts. A world below the world: frustrations, grudges, missed opportunities, an incalculable web branching with no return. There are buildings under buildings, streets meandering under streets, rivers and veins forming a murmuring nocturnal lattice. The world is the death of infinite unfulfilled futures.

Tom is dead.

He's on his third beer already. One Amber, one Old, then another Amber. He gobbles them down like water. He doesn't even recognise the taste anymore. Only this world is real, he says to himself. He clings to the flimsy shapes that fluctuate over the more real shadows beneath. He looks at his reflection in the window and his image seems more substantial to him than his own presence. There is the real Tom, a stranger watching him from behind glass. *Tom.* The name had meant something to her. Could it have been a coincidence? His mind forces himself to say yes. His stomach says no.

Tom is dead.

He should call—what's her name? Joanna, of course, Joanna... what an absurd sound! *Joanna, Tom...* By the fifth beer, things begin to fit back into their appropriate places. The shadows become still until they coincide with the everyday forms and disappear behind them. It's time to go. As he gets up from his chair, he realises how drunk he is.

Tom is dead. Somewhere, in some world, at some time.

He waits on York Street, the same place where he always waits. It is night and the street is almost empty. He doesn't remember which bus is his. Perhaps, if he stares at them long enough, the numbers will sound familiar. He's scared that she will appear again. He tries not to look across the street, but there's no one there, only the wind, and the mannequins who have changed their clothes, and the windows that shout, announcing Spring.

When he arrives at the house an hour later, he realises that something is out of place. The door is open and the lights in the living and dining rooms are on. It occurs to him that thieves have entered. However, they haven't touched anything.

The house receives him in silence. The stereo is on, also the television, but without volume. The upper part of the house is in darkness.

'Joanna?'

Most of the books are hers, all about yoga and cooking. Tom used to read a lot. There's a cold pizza on the kitchen counter. It rests on the pink tablecloth. The guitar that hasn't been touched in two years gathers dust. There's the lamp on the table, the arabesque vase he has always hated. Now this hatred seems ridiculous, as does everything he sees.

He is filled with an urge to run, to flee from this life. He realises it's not the first time he has felt this way. He has always felt like this. Yes, he would like to go. That's how it is every night when he returns to this place, the house, their house, his house, whatever.

An alarm buzzes in his head, high-pitched, searing. '*Joanna?*' Louder this time. There's no answer. He's suddenly very sober. The sound of his feet on the carpet is hollow, a vacuum in his ears. He heads upstairs. Whenever they argue, Joanna locks herself there, in the room, under the covers. But she has never expressed her discontent this way, leaving the door open, suddenly abandoning everything.

He climbs the stairs. Now, his feet sound deafening on the wooden steps. Invisible hands squeeze his neck and throat. He leans against the door frame. As his eyes adjust to the darkness, a silhouette emerges from the shadows. Behind that square cutout of the ordinary world lies the one they should be in—the unmade bed, the milky glow of the sheets, the half-open window. He contemplates his wife without knowing what to do. She conceals her face in her clenched hands, fully dressed, wearing the coveralls she uses to paint, blotted with stains of various colours.

After a while, she lifts her gaze, her eyes red and puffy, and directs it to the window. She hasn't noticed his presence yet, the presence of Tom. He heads towards her with great effort, fighting against the dense air like gelatin.

Joanna extends her hand and tears a bunch of paper tissues from a box on the bedside table. When she notices him, her throat expels a sigh, choked, like a distant cry, and her hand stalls halfway in the air. Her fingers tremble, suspended, squeezing the tissues. She studies him as though he were a stranger. It seems she will cry again, but she identifies him and some of the old Joanna returns. The everyday her.

He sits by her. After some clumsy groping, he puts an arm around her shoulders. He moves slowly to preserve the fragile calm, the precarious balance of Joanna swinging over the abyss. He waits for the room to accept his presence, for the air to circulate again, for the world to start breathing. When was the last time he made such a spontaneous gesture towards her? A gesture not of love but concern. That, at least.

He sits still and contrite until his arm hurts and begins to shake. The shuddering curtain is the only indication that time is passing. Soon the moon will rise over the row of pines, back to cosmic time. He opens his mouth, tries to say something, and falls silent. She is trembling. He draws her near and presses her cheek against his chest. To his surprise, she doesn't resist. They remain like that.

The light shifts, shadows move across the room on tiptoe, the tremor in their bodies slowly subsides. The first signs of a migraine squeeze his temples. It seems like the hangover is coming early.

Joanna speaks. 'I'm dead, Tom.'

It takes him a few moments to register the words. 'Dead? *How?* What do you mean?'

Her head turns and she stares at him through tangled hair, trying to recognise him again. Then her gaze drifts and is lost in the dark. Her words seem to come out from nowhere. 'I was driving back from Therese's, and I almost had an accident. Well, I *did* have an accident. God, Tom!' His name sounds unfamiliar, the name of someone else.

As she talks, he untwines her words into images, reconstructing her story in his mind. She's driving the Mazda through Frenchs Forest in northwestern Sydney. She's singing along to a Bon Jovi song on the radio, thinking about home and what she'd talked about with Therese.

The streets wind around the National Park in steep curves and dips. As she drives up an inclined, sharp bend, she sees a truck coming the other way, turning slowly and veering into her lane. Joanna slams on the brakes. The tires screech and the car vibrates, the steering wheel shaking in her hands. She swings to her left and manages to control the vehicle. Her heart jumps in her chest. She stops the car by the side of the road, digesting what had just happened.

For a moment, a vision clouds her view of the real world. The vision glows with a sharp feeling of anxiety, as if she has lived it before—or *should* have lived it. 'But this was not *déjà vu*, Tom. It wasn't *déjà vu* at all.'

Tom can see her. He sees her death behind his eyelids. Beyond some parapet of that curve, at the edge of a gorge, lies the destroyed car on fire and Joanna dying inside. Her skin burns and peels, an oppressive torment that corrodes skin and extinguishes consciousness. It's just a moment, like lightning. The liquid fire consumes the flesh and the muscles; the furious blast fills the surface of the bones. Everything ends there, in an eternal blink of an eye. The body does not respond, and everything turns to darkness.

She can see the dark like a screen in front of her eyes where jumbled afterimages flutter and fade, except there are no eyes anymore. The hazy reality stirs behind the silhouette of the truck, the red lights like little eyes looking at her, the trees still at night. She forces herself to blink, shakes her head and tries to wake up. *I am here, and everything's fine,* she repeats to herself.

They stay still. There is no moon tonight, just the artificial glow of the suburbs, a grimy yellowish light drowning among the shadows. Tom is afraid to turn on the light and see what's around him: the face of Samantha, Joanna, whoever. He lets time crawl, helplessly. He lets the night take them away. The shadows lengthen. In the window, the world is the same. Except it isn't.

ARRIVALS/ARRIBOS

They came with a dim notion of what awaited. During the eleven long months that preceded the journey, they tried, each in their own way, to envision the new country, but it was like trying to conceive Greenland or Uzbekistan. Even the surface of the moon managed to evoke a clearer, more familiar image. The photos, documentaries and brochures only aggravated the uncertainty. The pictures showed blazing sand beaches, vivid seas, clean and ultramodern cities, and red deserts so vast you could see the Earth's curvature. The distinctive fauna (the kangaroo, the lethargic koala, the unlikely platypus) seemed as unreal as the scribbles of a kindergarten god.

Every culture cherishes its own imaginary geography of the world. Certain names occasion prompt answers, a mix of prejudice and folklore. But Australia was a lacuna in the Argentinian imagination, a place that appeared as a combination of all possible places. And I wonder if this was the reason they chose to go there.

They follow the herd of travellers headed for the baggage carousels. Sleepwalking legs carry them through the network of corridors, beyond the garish light and shadowless spaces. Valeria drags their child, Sebastián, by the hand. Sebastián walks with short, feeble steps, watching the people and the adverts askance.

'Everything seems very modern,' Valeria says to her husband, Ernesto. 'They have escalators.'

Ernesto searches for local time on the arrivals screen. 2:39 pm—that makes it twenty to two in the morning back home. He must reset his watch, but there will be time for that.

Modern? It looks new, that's for certain, as if it had all been built yesterday, and probably it has been. There is no way of knowing. Everything is just for them, like a stage. The floors, carpets, columns—nothing can adhere to these surfaces and materials, designed for a perpetual transit that leaves no trace. Not the exhaustion, the fear, the anger.

Bernard Palissy was the first to leave. He was born in 1747 in Limoux, France, to a family of provincial nobility who had won, after the efforts of three generations, a place in the military aristocracy. In 1770 Palissy was appointed captain in the Spanish navy after Spain and France agreed to share their military forces. It was during this time that Bernard first heard of the Enchanted City from the mouth of the officers who had served in the American colonies.

Trapalanda, The White King, the City of the Caesars, El Dorado—all these stories seem to have common origins, and for more than two centuries they led adventurers, priests and fortune hunters deep into the inhospitable lands of the south in search of gold, silver and souls to save. Since the very beginning, legends and imaginary geographies, inherited from the Middle Ages, propelled the 'discovery' and looting of the continent.

Columbus wanted to reach Cipangu and Cathay, the lands Marco Polo and Mandeville had described. They were supposed to be overflowing with spices, gold and precious jewels, and home to dragons, devils, amazons, unicorns and mermaids. Soon after, Amerigo Vespucci described a fantastic trip in which he had seen mountains of gold and emeralds, and history rewarded him by giving his name to a new continent.

Argentina was colonised because of these stories and its very name derives from them. The survivors of the expedition of Solís, the first to enter the Río de la Plata, returned to Spain carrying rumours of a fabulous civilisation with mountains of solid silver and a city, El Rey Blanco, ruled by a monarch and covered in shining ornaments of precious metal.

Over time, the legend grew with a life of its own and spread across the region. It was said that the abundance of precious minerals in these kingdoms was so formidable that their inhabitants dined with utensils and dishes made of gold and silver. They lived in sumptuous buildings of carved mineral, encrusted with precious stones. Some said that the City was in the middle of two mountains, one of gold and one of diamond. The effulgence of its towers and roofs could be spotted from a long distance.

The people of the City were white, blond, blue-eyed. They spoke a language unintelligible to Spaniards and Indians alike. They were immortal, immune to disease. It was believed that the City was invisible to non-natives, but that it could be seen momentarily at dusk on Holy Fridays. Others said it was a wandering city that continually changed position. Those who wished to find it had to remain in one place long enough. The legend inspired a steady stream of failed expeditions. Palissy's was the last documented.

Time flows as in a feverish dream. The English language (spoken, whispered in passing, written, announced, flickering on screens) is a constant reminder that they are elsewhere. The signs enumerate a profusion of non-places: exits, bathrooms, doors, terminals, escalators, information. The child's hand is heavy and damp. She drags him, entranced by the ads that occupy entire walls and sell all kinds of seductive, strange products.

'Sure! Here everything is imported,' Valeria says to the walls. Ernesto squints at the life-sized images of peach-skinned models jumping at him, offering beer, underwear, credit cards—officious subalterns of an ethereal and over-lit Hell.

They reach the collection area and remain standing, lurking like fishermen at the waters, watching the suitcases, boxes and bags that swim by. Ernesto makes an observation: no two pieces of luggage are identical. How is that possible? One by one they identify their luggage, stacking it precariously on the cart. Four suitcases and two canvas bags are all that remain. They can hardly recognise them against the background of this alien landscape.

¿What is it doing here, our stuff? What are we doing here?

Any moment now, a demonic hand will plunge into the bath of the world and remove the plug.

In November 1776, Palissy went to Argentina under the command of Pedro de Cevallos, the new governor and supreme military commander of the recently created Viceroyalty of the Río de la Plata, the region comprising present-day Argentina, Uruguay, Paraguay, Bolivia and Perú.

Over the following year, Palissy served under Cevallos in campaigns across the eastern shore, regaining Portuguese positions. Then, as they moved across Río Grande, news came that the king of Portugal had died. His widow, the King of Spain's sister, took the throne. A treaty was signed and the Eastern band went to the Spanish, ending the campaign.

Palissy followed Cevallos to Buenos Aires. The city was establishing itself as the main access point from Spain, and the most important commercial and political centre in the American colonies. The harbour was also a frantic nest of smuggling involving the Dutch, English, French, Portuguese and North Americans.

Promoted to General, Palissy created his own regiment and led raids across the interior of the country to defend its borders against Indian attacks. Meanwhile, he gathered information, talking to the settlers and wanderers he came across. He befriended José de Vértiz, the successor to Cevallos, who recognised the importance of exploring Patagonia. Thus, an expedition was proposed with the aim of mapping the western regions, the strip at the foot of the Andes, and finding the city of the White King on the way.

In his head, night after night, brick by brick, invisible hands built houses of silver and gold. They shone so intensely in his dreams that the glare would often wake him up. Palissy sat in the dark, watching the afterglow of the city vanish on the horizon of his quarters. During the day he trained his men, preparing them for the savage vicissitudes of the pampas, and the cruel ice and heights of Patagonia. Perhaps the dream had started as a delirium of fame, fortune or royal titles, but now the vision was dragging in with its own momentum like the rapids of a river yet without a name.

They wait in the customs line, wrapped in a distant anxiety born from exhaustion.

Valeria shakes the boy's shoulder. 'Are you all right, dear?' Sebastián nods dimly. Who knows what's going on in that little head of his?

They watch the officials opening bags and grappling with suitcase latches. They finger the contents on long tables, sticking their hands in like dissectors examining internal organs. One of them takes a donkey toy, a souvenir of the Andean region, to his ear and shakes it. Valeria notices that some staff are letting people through without even touching their luggage. She directs the family to one officer who seems sympathetic.

The officer's gaze examines them, landing on Sebastián. A fleeting shadow swims past below his face. 'Nothing to declare?'

Valeria and Ernesto think for a moment and shake their heads unanimously. The official glances wearily at the luggage. He moves his hand, indicating the exit.

'Thank you, thank you,' sings Valeria. Ernesto lets his wife take care of the natives. So far, they look nice enough. Valeria speaks measured English, with exaggerated lip movements. For many months she has been practising and has composed a list of phrases to cover all eventualities. *Excuse me, how do I get to the city? We are looking for a hotel to stay in. We want it not to be too expensive.* They change money, get the name of a hotel, and collect free maps of Sydney.

After studying reports and several maps of the Viceroyalty's territories, General Palissy concluded that the city should be on the edge of Andean Patagonia, in today's province of Santa Cruz. The group's cartographer, Lieutenant Horacio Sánchez Donofrio, recorded in a chronicle the hardships that gradually undermined the expedition. The horses were the first to die and the men had to eat the raw meat quickly before it froze. Palissy is portrayed as a good military leader, inspiring the loyalty of his men even if it meant the doom of all. Day after day, watching the thickets and horizons, the gaze of the General acquired an intolerable deepness that pierced mountains, wind and the souls of men.

Donofrio recounts an anecdote that reveals something of Palissy's personality. When they were marching, Palissy used to look over his back. He watched the dust trails that people, horses and carts left in their wake. At night, after the men went to sleep, he stayed, staring at the smoke from the fires tickling the dark. The General told his subordinate that these things made him remember the white trail of ships cutting the surface of the waters. After that, Donofrio could not see the dust or smoke without thinking about water. The association was comforting and carried his mind away from the cold and exhaustion.

Of the seventy-two who departed, only five returned. And not much more is known about Bernard Palissy. The surname of my distant ancestor is the most present legacy of all the dead who accompany us. Bernard Palissy is merely a thread leading into a dense tapestry of ancient origin. Here the names are lost but a universal memory remains.

We know that Palissy married Amelié Bergsonier, the grand-daughter of French settlers belonging to another military family. Vertíz assigned him a comfortable position in Customs, and, at that point, Palissy vanishes from history.

Valeria inflates her lungs with the air of the new world, a humid and fresh air announcing rain. They move along the path aimlessly. Their gazes search for the city. In front of them, there is a parking lot. The four-level, cement structure seems as large as the terminal itself. On either side are sky and nondescript plains.

Ernesto pushes the cart along the crosswalk. It seems heavier by the second. He cannot recognise any of the cars. He has read that Australians like Japanese cars, which makes sense, considering the geographical proximity. The taxis are also Japanese. In comparison, the black-and-yellow taxis in Buenos Aires seem like funeral hearses. But remembering is a luxury. They need to find a taxi now. No dictatorship lasts forever.

Valeria checks the slip of paper with the hotel's details. The letters slide in front of her eyes, their meaning slipping out of reach, but she must be strong. She must be strong for Sebastián, who is looking fascinated at a group of people dressed in traditional African attire. They are the first black people he has seen outside of a TV. Valeria squeezes his hand, pulling him forward.

'You're sweating,' she says to her husband. 'Take off that jacket.'

It looks like it is the cart that is leading Ernesto. No wealth, no titles nor fame, just a decent life away from the past. He turns his head, contemplates his wife for a second and starts to squirm out of his jacket while pushing the pile of luggage.

'Aren't you hot, Sebastián? It is hot, right?'

'Where are the kangaroos, Dad?'

'Soon we will see them. They don't like to mingle with people.'

They join a queue of people pushing carts, dragging suitcases and carrying sports bags. The taxis form another queue.

Sebastián points to a cab waiting at the curb. 'Are these police cars, Mum?'

Valeria chuckles without breath. She taps him lightly on the neck. 'No, of course not. They are *taxis*, see? Taxis.'

The taxis swallow people and luggage, and one by one they tear off from the curb and disappear.

Get a house, find a job. Sebastián must go to school. He is already going to miss one year.

When their turn comes, the driver helps with the luggage. He wears a uniform: a short-sleeved shirt with shoulder flaps and black pants. He has dark skin, a thick beard and a funny hat like a cloth wrapped around his head. They stare at him, motionless.

'Do you want a ride or not?' he asks, pointing to the car, and the Palissys come back to life. Ernesto lifts a bag, but his arm fails and it falls on one side, making a metallic noise like clanging pots. Valeria's face shrinks. Were those her ornaments? She tries to remember the name of the country where people wear turbans.

There is a roar in the sky, and Sebastián looks up. A Boeing 747 rises in the air like a stuffed bird and its belly catches fire from the sun. They have come like this, in the stomach of a bird that now watches them from above as though they were ants.

Mum squeezes his shoulder. 'Let's go.'

Dad helps him onto the back seat. The child can do it alone and does not need help, but Dad is always in a hurry. Mum shows Sebastián a shaky smile, but her eyes do not smile. She pushes her soft and immense body against his, wedging him against Dad's sharp hip.

The door slams and Mum hands the driver the crumpled piece of paper.

My parents came to Australia to escape history, but history insisted on following them across oceans and continents. Now here I am, still pursued by its insomniac spectra, for whom time and space are one single moment and place.

END OF SEASON

For some reason, she preferred It as a man. She loved the obsidian eyes and the pensive dome of his skull. She loved the ripples of pale muscle stretched over his bones, his ribs, the hollows in his neck and cheeks. She loved the wholesome instrument of his sex nesting in his groin, with its intricate lace of purple veins and its unthinking eye of flesh.

But this *It*—It scared her sometimes.

As It clambered down from the ship, Calista felt the usual mixture of anticipation and fear. She was a junkie, she realised, addicted to the secretions of her own body, her excitement, her dreamy moods and bouts of anger.

The first thing she noticed was that It was older. Another season had passed. Already? She could see It was changing, becoming a *he* again. Probably a couple more days, a week at the most.

She stepped forth. 'Welcome home, Duncan,' she said, trying to inject some cheerfulness into her voice. 'Any action out there?'

Duncan halted in surprise, picking up her presence. It let out a low hiss, which she interpreted as a sigh of disillusion.

'Not much, eh?' she said.

Its multifaceted eye assessed her quickly, yet thoroughly. The gaze was like a beam of light searching a dark room. *Have you been naughty, Calista? Have you played in the labs while I've been away? Have you tampered with the machines?* But there were new corners in her soul now, secret places Duncan knew nothing of.

As Calista approached to kiss It, the gaze continued to search for something in her expression. What It was seeking was unclear. She only knew that one day the elusive sign would be found and that her time would then run out.

They fucked. Duncan's skin was cold after the trips, and his eyes were empty. Every time It returned, It brought a whiff of the Void, the tick-tocking of entropy home. Together, on the large low-g bed in the main bedroom, they rode the violent undercurrents and the vertigo of infinity. It was as if Duncan, after weeks of cruising through nothingness, was trying to make up for something, trying to soak up her human warmth in one gigantic intake, to reap it savagely out of her.

It cupped her breast in long purple-furred fingers. Its insides shivered under the vitreous skin. In Its hands, her breast became like a grail, a symbol of Duncan's longing to be a man again. But now there was something else, something she had never seen before. Duncan looked... *scared?*

She wrapped her legs around It and mounted It again. As they neared another climax, she pinned It to the bed and stilled Its movements until they both lay motionless. She liked to savour Its member inside of her, feel its pulsations, its rivers gorging with blood. Its sex became a part of her, an extension of her nervous system. Its pleasure was her pleasure, Its fear, her fear.

In those moments of stillness, she reached into her own Void that was also Its Void that was also the Void outside enfolding them, immense and uncaring and slowly engineering their deaths and the death of everything behind curtains of icy space and inexorable temporality.

The climax was always a disappointment, the wave of ecstasy too closely followed by a spasm of physical disgust and satiety. Her insides churned as her cells began to assimilate Its jism. But the queasiness quickly passed. And she was on again.

The welcoming fuck lasted almost two days. Duncan was almost a man by the time they finished. Its skin peeled back and the layers of Its exoskeleton came off in fragments. They stopped only to drink the food from the machines and clean the mess from Duncan's transformation. The magnificent sky presided over their ritual—because the Void can be beautiful sometimes.

The arc of Annubis D loomed above, slowly climbing across the vault of the ceiling until it took over the whole view. In be-tween orgasms, they became aware of the green surface of the empty planet staring down at them, gently streaked with streams of volcanic red and gas clouds of cobalt blue. As the station went about its orbit, the sight of Annubis D drifted away and the sky blackened again. One by one, the stars appeared, their tiny flames puncturing the distance. Then Annubis D appeared again and the whole cycle repeated itself.

They lay back, exhausted. The ritual welcomes became shorter each time. She remembered when they lasted for weeks. Duncan's energies seemed to be ebbing. It was a pity, for Calista felt the opposite: invigorated, younger, strong. It was as if his life was slowly being transferred to her.

'Will you take me with you next time?' she asked him.

He took a long time to answer. His gaze scanned the skies. 'You won't like it now. There are fewer things to see.'

'But I am alone in here.'

'You have the machines. And the library.'

'They're not enough.'

'Please, Cal. I am not in the mood for this.'

Things had been different a few seasons before. She'd been allowed to travel with him, helping out with the charting of the trips and the gathering of the sensoria. They cruised across the galaxies, disseminating clouds of exploring machines, tiny artificial eyes that hungrily hunted life and the sights of the universe. They made love and lay back afterwards looking at the grand spectacle of the Void, which had not seemed so threatening back then.

Sometimes they asked the computer to reprocess and eroticise the colours of the nebulae and moons, to record the drifting songs of radiation and channel them into their spines. Their fucks acquired a different quality, and Duncan and Calista became like one writhing pyre. They screamed, they hurt, they levitated and they crossed myriad forbidden dimensions.

Then the planets began to die down. There was still a lot of activity out there, but the reports were unequivocal: the gradual cooling off was noticeable everywhere, and it was increasing exponentially. She had seen some of the latest pictures, the sterile surfaces of rock, the grey twilights and burning oceans. She had felt the stings of ice through the recordings, the *hate* in the skies, the crying of the winds and the furious chemical battles on her skin. It was the first sign of the collapse, the vast inward movement of the Void that would culminate with the annihilation of time and identity. The thought seemed to distress Duncan a great deal, and he had asked her not to come with him anymore.

One day Calista decided to stop looking at the recordings. Instead, she visited the library and reworked the old sensoria, combining various tracks and making up her own planets, with large nomad cities of crystal and long-fingered birds sailing across the turbulent ether. Through the control of her electrical potentials, her memories and her thoughts, Calista could alter the recordings and make new ones. The places gradually disintegrated and became abstract accumulations of sensoria running over her body. Soon there was only one planet, the Calista planet, one desert of blue sands and many small suns dancing across the heavens. In her own small way, Calista could rewrite the universe, although she was powerless to avert its end.

'I am going to die one day, my honey. Soon,' Duncan said.

'What do you mean?'

'I will be no more. Not as I am now, anyway. My body will break up into fragments and join the lower strata of being.'

She understood, and the thought filled her with terror.

'Does that mean we won't be able to fuck anymore?'

He smiled and averted his gaze. It was good to see him smile. But when he looked at her again there was that expression on his face, the same one she had seen in It earlier that evening.

After they washed, she followed him into the labs. Or rather, *he* followed her. The deterioration of his body was becoming apparent. He walked slowly and she frequently had to stop to let him catch up. He stooped, and his eyes regarded her strangely. But she was glad to have Duncan, *him* again. Her father. Her lover.

They halted at the doors of the lab and she eyed him inter-rogatively. As a girl, the world of the station had seemed endless and full of wonder, and the labs had been one of her favourite places to play. But her world had narrowed considerably since then, and she had come to regard her place of birth with a kind of superstitious terror.

'We are going to go in,' he said, looking at the metal door. 'We will check how our babies are going.'

The door opened soundlessly. They moved through the corri-dors past sealed doors until they arrived at a spacious and dimly lit room. At the centre of the room, there was a row of cylindrical glass containers. Inside the containers, floating in a clear blue liquid, were dozens of human embryos joined to machines by thick umbilical cables.

Duncan leaned over the terminals and scanned the screens of data. He frowned and began to type something on one of the keyboards. As he worked, some of his youthful vitality returned, and the lines of his face seemed to disappear.

'Shit,' he said finally. 'This is no good.'

'Our success rate is optimal,' the computer responded. 'Especially if we consider the circumstances.'

Duncan glanced at her, then back at the screen. 'They are deformed,' he said. 'Dumb and sick children. Get rid of them all. Except maybe for number *nine*. He seems to be doing okay. Replace the cultures and start again.'

A wheezing sound was issued from the equipment surrounding the containers. In unison, needles emerged from the top of the tanks and descended onto the soft shells of the babies' skulls. The computer pumped in the poison, a thick brown stream that flowed into the tiny bodies and dissolved them.

'Why did you make me?' she asked him as the remains were flushed from the containers.

Duncan kept staring at the monitors. 'You will know in due time,' he said, finally.

She didn't have to wait long. Although their routine continued as normal, she could tell Duncan was agitated, that things were not the same. He was absent for days, working at the lab. He had made some androids to entertain her, but soon she got bored with them. She ended up destroying the stupid things, one by one, cutting their heads off with a laser while they continued to fuck her, then ordering them to form a queue and march into the nearest garbage chute.

'I want to live to the end,' he confessed one day, after an unusually tender succession of fucks. 'Do you understand that?'

'No,' she said.

'Please try. I am getting old, and it is necessary that you understand. It is your destiny.'

'I can try.'

'It is a waste, you know? All these millions of years of evolution for nothing. When the Big Crunch comes, I will have my revenge in the name of every sentient being that ever existed. I will go down that fucking hole laughing. You understand?'

'No. Things are born, they grow and die. No big deal. You taught me that. It's a hard thing to learn.'

'It is your destiny,' he said, as if not listening.

The end of season arrived one morning, not long after that conversation. She disconnected from the library machines and felt it, heavy in her bones, as if the marrow in them had turned to lead. She sought her own image in the polished concave walls of the library room. A part of her understood. A part of her had always *known*. And when she couldn't find her reflection on the walls, she rushed out through the corridors and searched for it on the windows of the ship and on the metallic surfaces of the machines.

She spotted it on one of the com terminals, a distended face lying on the surface of the inactive screen. She looked at her image for a long time. She looked different. *Older?* No, that wasn't it. She looked like... *him.*

She was suddenly very cold. Duncan was on a trip, and for the rest of the afternoon, she sat without moving, waiting for him. She knew he had to come soon. She thought of killing herself but knew the machines would not let her do it. She knew so many things that day. It was all so clear.

He climbed down from the ship. His movements were wooden and mechanical. In his eyes, Calista saw boiling volcanoes, cumulus of dead gas. But mostly she saw nothingness, one infinite flat field of no movement, no time and no thought. He was older, much older. His joints were tangled knots and his eyes were sunken in folds of yellow flesh. His legs were bent and carried him unsteadily. His hair was nearly all gone, only two wisps of white left floating on his temples.

Duncan assessed her. But he couldn't hold her stare for long. He knew. 'Come, Calista,' he said.

Later, in the main bedroom, as she lay on the bed naked, Duncan wheeled in the machine. It was a machine she had never seen before, a floating contraption of thin needles and tiny eyes with an insectoid stomach of polished chrome. He fumbled with the controls, punching a code on a tiny keyboard, then cursed and punched it again.

The machine shook and unfolded. Spheres of crystal gyrated in the air, held by tendons of aluminium. The machine came to life and looked at them, appraised them, studied them. She could feel its stare weighing her bones, measuring her internal liquids, listening to her breathing, her thoughts, the flow of her blood. Duncan extracted two thin tubes from the body of the machine and motioned for her to stand up. She hesitated for a moment.

But then she obeyed, knowing that it was better than the alternative, better than resisting, better than being alone or—worse—uncreated. Better than growing old.

Duncan drove the tip of the tube into the base of her skull. Then he did the same thing to himself, probing his neck with infirm fingers until he found the exact spot.

They lay on the bed. His skin was brown and hung in folds. His flesh seemed to be detaching itself from his muscles. She held his penis in her hand and massaged it tenderly, looking for a twitch, the beginning of an erection. It was slow at first, but she orchestrated everything carefully, attacking his centres of pleasure, driving his old body onwards and onwards.

Then she could feel what he was feeling, and she could tell by his eyes that he could feel what *she* was feeling too. They were locked in a feedback loop. There were no secrets now. He felt his own rugged skin through the touch of her hands. She felt the wet apex of her own labia, magnified and distorted by his lust. She saw the terror, the naked terror of a caged beast glowering in his bloodshot eyes. She *felt* it and added her own. The juice of carnal electricity became a rapid, then a vicious and deafening waterfall. The intensity of the emotions threatened to overflow their bodies, to burst through their skins—to *kill* them.

Their confused and fragmented bodies soon approached the climax, the final little death. Duncan's member was breaking, growing, hurting. The muscles of her sphincter were contracting and expanding like the lips of a starved mouth. Throughout the experience, they could feel the presence of the machine presiding distantly over the affair and computing their responses.

The world disappeared. *Goodbye, Duncan.* She wasn't sure if she said this or if she merely thought it. It was the same thing now.

He woke up and couldn't move. It took him a few moments to locate his body, a thing bereft of feeling or movement hanging from his neck. He knew something was amiss. There was pain, a pain he could not associate with any area of his body in particular. It came in waves, then it trickled, then poured in again.

The view was familiar. It was the Void again, as seen through the dome of the master bedroom. The stars were staring at him. The dying stars.

For a while, nothing happened. He tried to remember. But it hurt to do so. It was like touching a sore, bruised membrane. And he could only gather small flashes, a face, a series of landscapes— meaningless fragments.

There was another presence in the room. He was aware of it long before he saw the lean and long-haired figure walk into his field of vision. He couldn't recognise her at first. And when he did, there was a torrent of memories. It all came back to him. He remembered. And he understood.

'It worked, Calista,' the woman said. It was not a question.

He tried to speak but could not find his mouth. He felt sick, every cell in his body spinning and disoriented. The woman approached and inspected him closely, maybe wondering if he was alive at all. He saw the face he had seen earlier on the dead screen of the com unit. The woman was himself—*her*self.

He saw a hand, his own hand, rising of its own accord. The hand was brown and decrepit. He felt the vertigo of the new (*old*) body weighing him down, writhing inside as if trying to dislodge its new host. The index finger twitched weakly once, and then the hand dropped out of sight.

Duncan was saying something to him, but the meaning of the words slipped through his mental grasp.

'…atoms and flowers… alarm… but… nigh is… like the cumulative… beautiful… strong body… I will… do you… thank you… die… vanity and pride… Adam and Eve… for nothing… future… Fuck them.'

Then Duncan stopped speaking as if realising that her words were not getting through. She looked at Calista for what seemed an eternity.

It was good, Calista thought. *While it lasted.*

Duncan frowned for a moment, and then she smiled. Had she heard him? Calista hoped so.

'Do you want to go now?' she said. She had to repeat the question a few times.

In a little while.

Duncan nodded.

'I'll give you twenty minutes.'

She turned to leave, then halted. 'Goodbye,' she added.

See you.

He was lying there, thinking of nothing in particular. He felt a warm liquid rush entering his spine and remembered he was still connected to the machine. Some of the pain retreated and the colours became sharper.

Thank you.

As the station continued on its orbit, the first glimpses of Annubis D entered the bottom corner of the dome. The atmosphere was like the halo on the head of a giant angel.

When his time was up, the machine issued a command and another rush of liquid, of a very different nature, flooded his spine.

Calista closed his eyes.

COOLING DOWN

Others collect stamps, train tickets, *Star Wars* figurines. Michael Michelos collects entropy.

'Mylers & Morloch is about Big Ideas,' he tells the team. 'We deal in Love and Death, Chaos and Cosmos. We are a company at the cutting edge of creativity and innovation, and we are not afraid to tackle the Big Picture.'

His wife Michaela is beginning to seriously worry about him. His son Michel, on the other hand, tolerates his father's eccentricity with a poker face. But then again, as Michaela always says, he doesn't have to live with it.

'Entropy,' Michael intones, raising his arms in a gesture calculated to appear spontaneous, 'is the sexiest, most important of all modern ideas. It is hard not to be seduced by its poetic implications, its sense of tragedy and finality. But nowadays entropy seems to have become a relic in the museum of ideas, only of interest to us survivors of the Computer Age because it provided the basis for information theory. But we should keep in mind that without entropy there would be no Einstein and no quantum physics.'

He pauses to gauge the effect so far. It's a small group, only five of his top staff. He glances at Michelle's brief on his desk and tries for the twentieth time that day to commit their names to memory. Micheal Miacael and Mick Mechial from the Executive Board; Mike Leachim and Micall Mikaelos from Marketing & Promotions; and Kim Miclel, Head Creative Consultant.

'The truth of entropy, my dear colleagues, is of a staggering simplicity. Energy flows from places of high concentration to places of less concentration. Things always seek to even out, to dissipate into a state of equilibrium from which no further activity can be generated. This single principle is behind everything that happens in the universe.'

Of course, the notion of collecting entropy is a contradiction in terms. Entropic processes are evanescent and encompass all phenomena in the universe. Michael knows this well and that is why he is content with hoarding scientific memorabilia. Besides, the very act of collecting is entropic because it concedes that the past was more valuable and richer in creative possibilities.

Over the years he has accumulated an impressive collection of original manuscripts and first editions by Helmholz, Carnot, Lord Kelvin and others. His most prized possessions are an original scribble by James Prescott Joule (an early sketch of his famous experiment demonstrating the equivalence of heat and other forms of energy) and a rare first edition of *On Different Forms of the Fundamental Equations of the Mechanical Theory of Heat* by Rudolph Clausius, published in 1865 and containing the original mathematical definition of entropy. They cost him a small fortune.

Michael Michelos spends a lot of time in his studio, staring at equations he can barely decipher and waiting for an epiphany. The idea has pursued him ever since he first encountered the laws of thermodynamics at university. It's what he remembers best from his failed attempt at becoming a scientist. Michel often brings back items for his father's collection from his overseas trips, and

Michaela complains that Michel is just indulging Michael. As a freelance advertising consultant, Michel's work is in high demand around the globe, and his father is proud of him. He only wishes this sense of pride was reciprocated.

'Entropy is sexy because it is about desire and fate, hubris and life's final betrayal. So the aim of my campaign is to celebrate the ephemeral beauty of consumption, to say to customers everywhere: it's okay, get that tie, grab that bunch of flowers for the wife, make that deposit on a new car. We need to seize the precious and transient nature of life.'

Of course, Michaela doesn't understand. She also works in advertising, as a creative for Ormloch & Myers, so they compete personally and professionally. Advertisers have no time for lofty metaphysical speculation. All they care about is how to turn a lifetime of mortgage repayments into an irresistible commodity. Yesterday, for instance, Michael spent the entire afternoon in a meeting to decide what colour of swimwear would go best with this season's hot new sports car, the MM Motors Michaelo. The promotional samples came in two colours, mustard green and ocean grey. As far as Michael can remember, last year's models also came in these same colours.

After the usual deliberation with the accountants, the team opted for the standard approach: languidly voluptuous super-model in skimpy (mustard green or ocean grey) bikini, sun-glasses, martini, reclined on the bonnet (mustard green or ocean grey) in a desert or symbolically equivalent location. Then came a protracted discussion before they settled on ocean grey for both car and girl.

Michael works the room like a pro (three decades of practice that feel like many lifetimes). The signs are unpromising. That's fine, it's part of the build-up. Let them enjoy their false sense of confidence. Let them be *bored* even, just in time for the coffee trick.

Michael ambles to his desk, reaching for a cup of steaming black coffee and a jug of milk. This unexpected action has the desired effect of jolting his audience. From the corner of his eye, he glimpses a head straightening, a pen flicking.

'As I stir in the cold milk, we can see entropy at work, ensuring the even temperature of my drink. Each drop represents another tiny and irreversible step towards the final stasis of everything.' Pause to sip from the coffee, stone cold already; he swallows the grimace. 'The dynamics of heat and gravity, the turbulence of clouds, the motions of the wind. A child's ball rolling down a sloping footpath, smoke scattering in the air, the tender coolness that descends on your cheeks in the evenings of early spring. The Second Law explains why we gravitate towards paths of least resistance, why we fall in love, why we eagerly embrace the most meaningless activities, all in search of psychic balance.'

This morning, on the radio—had he heard that song before? And why think of this now, in the middle of selling his campaign to the team? Changing stations randomly, he heard the same song, or *almost* the same song. Is it like that every morning or has he just noticed it? In fact, he can hear it now… wait, it's a ringtone. The woman to the right—Micall or Kim? She's putting on the blankest of faces and trying to appear innocent, like someone who's just farted. You can see she's dying to take the call.

'The Second Law indicates that the universe tends towards chaos and disorganisation. That is, entropy increases with each breath of dissipated energy. Yet the popular imagination pictures this chaos as a busy, dynamic mess, a place full of activity. People think of chaos in romantic terms, but the scientific understanding of entropy suggests precisely the opposite.'

Michael likes to think he's doing this to give some creative output to his obsession. He's taking on this year's concept campaign, which the company organises with the aim of advertising itself. The campaign centres on an abstract theme, promoting values that Mylers & Morloch would like to be associated with in the minds of its clients. Entropy, Michael thinks, is a good value. It is about Energy and Truth.

'Chaos, however, is not activity but *rest*. It is sameness, not difference. An increase in entropy means the flattening out of differences towards an even spread of energy. Things cease to move and strive, and they begin to look like one another. Chaos is not a productive state but an inert, monotonous expanse, like a huge cup of cold coffee.'

While his colleagues digest the pitch, his assistant Michelle passes around coffees, pastries and cigars. Michael hates this part. He used to remember things. Kim, Micall and Michelle are hard to tell apart with their short, back-combed hair and sleeveless, ocean-grey dresses. Micheal, he thinks, is the one to the right, with the mustard-green, Italian-cut suit. Mick and Mike have always favoured ocean grey, but he can't tell who is who. Perhaps he should just point at them.

Michael Michelos listens to the reactions of his colleagues. Identical smiles hang at the corners of identical lips. His gaze wanders across the cityscape, the grey skyline crowded with skyscraping corporate blocks. Myloch & Morers, Morl & Myler, Lochmore & Ymors; the bright-green neon logos are the only way to tell the buildings apart. Although he's been working here for as long as he can recall, his head often reels at the sight of all that glass and steel, the convoluted network of mergers and partnerships stretching as far as the eye can see. He has not lost his sense of wonder, at least. Most of these corporations are subsidiaries of Mylers & Morloch or ventures in which the company is a major shareholder. But nobody remembers who came first or who merged with who. He collects entropy and only time will tell.

It seems that, while his mind is wandering, the discussion has turned into an argument. Mick or Micheal is raising his voice, saying something about problems with the budget, the layoffs due to the recent acquisition of Ymlers & Morlch. Risky idea... The others nod their heads in unison. The air is thick and Michael (or is it Mick?) has trouble breathing. Somewhere in those equations... We can do the campaign, yes, but we have to cut corners, you understand, a reasonable point. We have to rethink, adapt.

Finally, Kim or Micall suggests they scale it down a bit. And that they should begin by considering what colour of swimwear will go better with entropy, mustard green or ocean grey.

'THE CONSORTIUM MUST DIE', THE SUICIDE GHOST SAID

They've surely done a good job on the ghost.

'Just look at *it*, Roop, like a million *bucks!*' Fred Thunder turns in the plushy seat to face the ghost. 'The *suit* must've set them back two *grand*. What *is* it, Guccee? How *are* they *so* well-funded?'

The limo cruises in stealth-mode down New South Head Road toward Watson's Bay. High clearance beams freeze the other cars on the spot, making room for the CoreCorp vehicle.

'Hugo Boss,' Rupert Murdoch spits. He looks quite cheery having cheated one hell of a headline-grabbing death. 'The shoes are Gucci and they don't match. Proof that money can't buy taste.'

They cruise through pretty places with pretty names like Point Piper, Hermit's Place and Rose Bay while occupants seethe inside their stranded vehicles trying to glimpse the limo. You can tell the ghost has never been to these parts and is trying hard not to look at the pretty things, the harbour, the tree-lined streets.

The ghost should be dead, deader than it already is. The first reaction from the boys was to tear it apart and rape what was left of it, but Murdoch sniffed a potential high-hitter here—he's still got that journalist's touch. That's why Fred Thunder's here too. He's the King of the Stream.

Thunder leans close. 'At *least* they could've sent us a *woman*. We could've had some *fun*.' Thunder speaks like he's always in front of the cameras, emphasising words arbitrarily to some obscure effect. It secretly annoys Murdoch. 'Feel these seats, synthetic *baby* seal. Anything washes off them.'

But the public likes his tantrums and the way he punches his guests on his stream until they bleed all over the teleprompters. CoreCorp's pumped a lot of juice into his products. Thunder even has his own action figure coming out next quarter.

Murdoch smirks. 'Are you sure it's not a woman?' He waits for Thunder's brown-nosing laughter to subside. 'What do you reckon? An expose? A special investigation? Page three girl? You got the exclusive, Fred. Don't let me down.'

'The secret funding *trail* of the terrorists!'

'We don't call them that now.' They change the term whenever the techs glimpse the tiniest lunge in the Attention Span Index. Murdoch turns to Wall. 'What are they called now? I forget.'

Wall, the fourth, last and aptly named occupant of the limo, snaps out of a reverie. He looks like a Russian cyborg except he's not Russian. His massive frame seems hardly human, a mountain of flesh or stone, a Sphinx. Something you don't fuck with.

'The Shits,' Wall says, looking at the pretty colours. The back of the containment blocks holds the largest screen on Earth. CoreCorp owns it and Murdoch's very proud of it. The advertising revenue ejaculating from it should be enough to buy off the Consortium if only they'd let him.

'The *Shits!*' Fred echoes. All ghosts are Shits but not all Shits are ghosts. 'Hey Wall, are *you* sure it's neutralised?'

Wall's ocular globes pivot in their respective sockets, acquiring the target: Fred Thunder. 'Can't hurt a tiny teeny-weeny girl fly.'

As they ascend the winding streets, they catch sight of the ocean, where the price of real estate and the severity of security measures soar proportionally. This is the land of minus zero tolerance, well to the right of the Chasm. The high clearance shield shoos away drones, deactivates mines and neutralises early warning response systems. No one's on the streets, and the houses are in darkness. The whole place seems like an abandoned disaster area.

Wall himself spotted the ghost in the crowd as it approached the barrier at the end of the premiere. Incompetent idiots. Couldn't they just *see* the rat face with their own eyes? The thing screams *ghost* to the four winds, smells *ghost* from miles off. The thing shivering on the seat and staring uncomprehendingly at the most expensive advertising on the planet is literally a walking bomb, with explosive compounds tweaked right into the biochemistry of its cells. Smart catalysts can turn the locked-in triglycerides and phospholipids into volatile substances that leave a crater visible from the moon. You can hide the trigger compounds anywhere: chewing gum, a can of Coke. One sip, *kaboom*.

It's unbelievable how the ghost managed to walk undetected. Once, the Chasm marked the boundary of a real place, or rather a series of scattered places hidden from the public mind: refugee camps, slums, settlements, ghettos, detention centres, the Outlands of course, and all the polluted real estate you can't mine or otherwise profit from. But the Chasm is everywhere now, weaving in and out of people, *in between* them, zigzagging across streets and fence-lines. It marks imperceptible, ever-shifting boundaries.

Two people standing three steps apart will not see each other because of the Chasm. It's great if you're in the security business, which is currently 23% of CoreCorp, but one slip through the Chasm can have Hollywood consequences.

Case in point: the ghosts. Undetectable, anonymous, non-existent. Generic genetics, non-specific data points that slip under biometrics. Facial recognition, retina scans, gait analysis, background checks—you name it. It only triggers false ID or just a blank. No profile, no prints. The ghosts are a new breed of data, destitute in a global order that has installed the state of exception as the universal rule.

Murdoch strongly believes that the solution is universal ID. Microchipping, barcode on your forehead, whatever. Good business too, but the zealot Right is always muddying the pond with that whole Antichrist thing. The Christian neocons may be his allies and good customers, but Jeezus they can be a splinter in the balls sometimes.

'We're going to make you a star, no-name. Provided you open that mouth for once and say something we can broadcast.' Murdoch looks at the ghost as if he's honestly waiting for a reply.

Thunder chips in. 'What are you, *scared*?' The ghost stares at them, shivers. 'Does it even speak *Engleesh*?'

Murdoch tries his version of nice. 'You must've heard about Fred Thunder. He's got a successful daily stream, syndicated column, PA profile. Yes, you can program your wearable to talk like him. Don't you have media where you come from? All that virgin market, all those wasted consumers! Anyway, this to my right is Wall, real name Wallace. I once saw Wall whack an insurgent with a flick of his wrist. He drove the guy's nose-bridge into his brain and it shot out his ear. They were protesting about something. Rights, love, justice.'

'Yeah, Boss. You can *see* the footage on my *toobe* stream. Wall is *not* a killing machine, he's a *fucking* killing machine!' It seems that Thunder will touch the ghost any moment. 'And you *must* have heard of Rupert *Murdoch*. He's the one they *sent* you to kill.'

They're all a bit jumpy. Only two months ago, the Shits had their first home run with a ghost like this one decked with biostealth explosives. Todd Schneizer, CEO of ZoeSys and member of the Consortium of Five, was DNA'd from a charred memento the size of a SD card. They tried to hush-hush the whole thing but it didn't work. They couldn't just pretend the top five floors of 432 Park Avenue had *not* dematerialised in a puff of smoke.

Murdoch watched defencelessly as his 30% of VitaEterna, Schneizer's star gig, plunged into the void like a faulty space shuttle. He had no choice but to do what he always does: drown what's left of public consciousness in screaming commentary and endless looped footage. Thunder spent like eight feeds enraged about nothing else.

Now the audiences have forgotten, and most people just go *Schn-who?* Enter Velissa Xin-Lin, better known as *that* woman, who's taken Schneizer's place and become the most powerful female on the planet; well, besides Gina Rothschild, although no one thinks of that immobile lump of morbid hyper-obesity as female. Xin-Lin now controls the most powerful pack of technologies in human history: Indefinite Senescence (IS).

It's true that the Consortium is supposed to represent the most influential industries on what's left of the planet—Resources, Banking, Biotech, Media, Military—but without IS there is no Consortium. It pains him to admit that he's been upstaged by a woman, or *woman* as Thunder would say. He, Rupert Murdoch, has been entrusted with the vital job of keeping people stupid enough to buy what the other members of the Consortium are selling. Now they're all biotech junkies craving VitaEterna. Murdoch himself turns 156 next summer. And if Schn-who isn't selling, Xin-Lin sells even less.

'I shouldn't take it personally but I do,' Murdoch blurts. He's getting excited. It must be the cog extension chips playing up, making him think aloud. 'The Shits want me dead for the crime of being successful. For having built an empire from humble beginnings through sustained effort and merit. For trying to hold on to what is rightfully *mine*. The Shits are going to make sure that Indefinite Senescence does not perpetuate existing power structures. After all, it isn't murder to kill someone who is rightfully dead is it?' One thing Murdoch has to admit, though: having nothing to lose makes a formidable enemy out of anyone.

'Wall, are you recording this?'

Suddenly all blood drains from his face. The support system reacts quickly. Automated straps wheeze into place. Needles zoom out of the wearable and drive into his flesh, pumping him full of Life® again. As the drugs hit, an image of Xin-Li's face shoots into his mind. She's sneering. *What would Biotech be without Pharmatech?* Xin-Li is rumoured to be ninety years old but looks twenty-five. With her shiny, bald, egghead and retro sci-fi fashion sense, she looks like a cancer survivor from outer space. Although that transhuman holier-than-thou chic is all the rage among biotech corporatives nowadays, Murdoch suspects she's trying to impose World Socialism on everyone.

'For fuck's sake,' he shouts. 'She's a card-carrying *commie*.'

Wall keeps a stern eye on him, recording, while Thunder tries to hide his glee at the old man's tantrums. As the drugs hit, an image of Xin-Li's face shoots into his mind. Flashback from their last meeting. She's sneering.

You don't understand how tech works, Rupert. There is always a way around it. When you design a system, you also design its destruction, a way to cheat the system. When you design the airplane, you design the airplane crash and the hijacking. And when you design Life®, death is part of that Life®. Just like natural life. We can only slow it down a little, but sooner or later the cancer and mutations will start bursting like popcorn out of all your bodily orifices. The Greeks knew it: technology goes with *nature, not* against *it.*

Murdoch has some fuzzy affection for the Chinese. He even married one, Wendy-*whatshername?* It was a failed attempt to extend his dynasty there. The Chinese are serviceable and make good consumers, but they've also bought everyone's debt. And they're *communists*, although it's not polite to mention this.

He feels much better now that Pharmatech's here. Seriously, in this context, the increasing radicalisation of *that* woman's discourse is of great concern.

When the State of Exception becomes more dominant than the Rule it supposedly suspends, then the system will be eaten from within

by its own contradictions. Face it: Capitalism is a form of parasitism.
We are all parasites. We can't eat the host or we'll die with it.

Murdoch stares out the window, trying to regain his dignity.
The limo is cruising back down through Old South Head towards
the CBD. This part of Sydney is just as he remembers it. And it
looks better without people. Now they're heading back to head-
quarters, back to Holt Street to feed the ghost to the journos and
the masses.

'You're not going to say anything, are you?' The ghost looks
at him blankly and it occurs to him that it's blind. 'Wall, tell the
ghost here the secret of my success.'

As Wall's neck gyrates on its axis, you can hear the strands in
the thick log of muscle tear and regrow. He recites from beyond.
'It's easy to make people believe anything as long as you hammer
it down their throats enough. And people believe whatever makes
them happy.'

They've entered the Safe Zone. They zoom down Elizabeth
and swerve into Holt where the gates let them inside the heart
of Murdoch's Australian media operation. It should make him all
warm and fuzzy but it doesn't.

The limo halts. Guards and the usual cohort of arse lickers
flock to the vehicle like raging prepubescents.

Inside the vehicle no one moves. It's a strange moment, like
time has stopped. It lasts but a second and then something flickers at the corner of Murdoch's vision.

A loud dry crack.

Amazing, he thinks. Brain tissue runs down Fred Thunder's
shattered face. His eyes are wide open and in shock, flickering, as
if they want to jump out of their sockets before the gooey mass
occludes them. In one elegant ballerina movement, the security
agent, with his massive hand, has squeezed Thunder's skull like
an egg. The grey *stuff* looks like mechanically separated *chicken*
three months out of date. Thunder had no time to even whimper.
The nerves that would have allowed it were snapped at the source.

One eyeball dipped in brain rolls out of sight on the baby seal carpet. The ghost has moved out of the way and is actually frowning. Wall has that look on his face. He's uploading the whole thing in real-time to the *toobe*.

'Who,' Murdoch mutters stupidly, '*who* is it? Who did it? Jeezus, *fuck!*' Out the window, the crowd approaches in awful slow motion. The ghost looks at Murdoch, its face one silent question mark.

Wall pops open a can of Coke. 'Sorry not sorry, Boss. Just business, nothing personal.' He gurgles down the whole can while crushing it in his hand. With the other hand, he shows Murdoch the screen of his device.

Murdoch sees an anime version of Velissa Xin-Li winking her huge eye at him. A high-pitched squeal is looped to a Babymetal riff: *Thanks for shopping at VitaEterna, pigfucker.*

There's a bubbling, fizzy sound coming from inside Wall's body. The ghost is desperately fumbling at the door.

Before his component atoms scatter across a three-block radius, the last thought of Rupert Murdoch is something odd.

You actually have a nice voice. I should have put you on the Stream.

BECOMING

His new nature took over in phases. One did not become a machine overnight. It began by suppressing certain basic functions and reconfiguring others. Perception and motor skills were the first to undergo recalibration. His movements became stark, economic. By the end of this phase, he would spend most of his time motionless, standing very straight in a corner of the main room. At night he sat stiffly on a chair against the wall, perhaps a concession to a frail trace of humanity. As he switched to energy-saver mode, his mothers, Yoon and Anya, took advantage of the lapse to prop his head with pillows and comfort him. They took turns to give him hugs, whisper loving messages, caress his hair.

Even offline, Arlo resisted their ministrations. In the mornings, he played at being a cleaning robot for he wasn't sure what kind of machine he would like to be. Perhaps one day he could be a personal assistant and draw up dietary plans for his owners. He wiped the benches with repetitive circular movements, and he vacuumed and shook the rugs. He surveyed the contents of the fridge and memorised long shopping lists. At the end of the day, he recited a report on the duties he'd carried out and then announced he was waiting for further instructions.

Yoon and Anya felt hopeless. It was horrifying to watch. They tried to make him talk, to retrieve some dregs of humanity. His responses were algorithmic. He insisted his name was 673B964WZ. The more he repeated it, the more his mothers called him by his human name, trying to stoke his memory and bring Arlo back. Perhaps they could make him angry. There is nothing more human than anger, except perhaps vanity. Arlo withstood their efforts. He was too efficient, too incorruptible a machine.

One day he refused to eat. It marked the beginning of the second phase, another needless flesh function shut down. The women insisted that he sit at the table for breakfast, lunch and dinner. They pushed food at him, all his favourites, including seaweed cakes and strawberry-flavoured protein bars. Arlo sat straight, his hands hovering above the table, staring at them in turn. Then he reverted to default mode, his gaze fixed ahead on a point below the sink.

Yoon and Anya researched online. They listened to podcasts and watched documentaries. It was a worldwide phenomenon spreading like a virus. It affected mostly children and teenagers between the ages of eight and twenty-three, but adults, increasingly, were joining the trend. Fantasising about being machines, they became withdrawn and refused to be schooled or to work. Some stared at screens, acquiring data. Others became domestic robots, devoted to cleaning and household chores. Deaths were on the rise, mostly because of accidents, as youngsters attempted superhuman tasks. Twenty per cent starved to death or collapsed from heart failure due to exhaustion.

Yoon began to disguise human food as machine food. She added olive oil and colourant to water. It looked like something a machine would ingest. She mashed potatoes and minced meat to make a kind of porridge that could be shaped into pellets.

'The optimal number of pellets is twelve,' Yoon told Arlo, 'introduced every eight hours for correct machine functioning.' She intoned as dryly as she could, tuning to the machine mindset while tears clumped in her throat. She was always crying, ever since this thing had started.

Their efforts to bring him back were exhausting and placed a heavy burden on their relationship. Old recriminations came to the surface like bloated corpses in high tide. Yoon and Anya worked from home like everyone in their social class. They rearranged their schedules so they could take turns watching Arlo. Anya was an IT consultant for a prestigious communications company. She was constantly connected and the work left her drained. Yoon was an industrial engineer for a large corporation specialising in cooling systems. She worked on large projects where the modules were divided up among hundreds of workers. She never knew what she was helping to build. Perhaps it was some horrible machine like a missile system or a death ray.

Each day, they had three hours together when their off-time overlapped. Yoon was tired from the night shift and Anya was drowsy from waking up and never getting enough rest. They were never sure whether to have breakfast or dinner, so Arlo began to serve them a meal that could perform both functions: bean curd and vegetable fibre, mixed with citric juice. The silences stretched longer and deeper. They hardly touched each other anymore, and their rare incursions into the City became rarer. It would be good to sleep tirelessly like a machine. Fresh and cold. No thoughts, no dreams.

They could keep Arlo fed but feared the long-term consequences of being a machine. The months passed and Arlo showed the same unwavering commitment to his role. As his deep learning system refined its data sets and developed interactional skills, he engaged in more fluent conversations. He imitated basic human gestures, like a smile or an expression of surprise. His mothers sank deeper into despair. They no longer hid their tears from him or each other. Yoon was the most fragile. She became depressed and angry, and she cried for hours. She refused to take her pills because she said they made her like a machine: unresponsive, passive, soulless.

'There will be a cure,' said Anya. 'They'll work it out. We have to keep watching.'

Eighteen months passed and Yoon could not take it anymore. She left without saying goodbye. Anya found a note scribbled on her tablet in unintelligible writing. A weird choice of media, handwriting. An empty gesture, Anya thought, reminding ourselves that we're human.

With Yoon gone, Anya's decline was swift. She became distracted, apathetic and neglected her personal hygiene. She made too many mistakes at work and was sacked. One morning she decided to become a machine too. She had nowhere else left to go. She sat in a corner and watched Arlo perform his daily routine. The mother's departure did not appear to affect the boy-machine. He vacuumed and inventoried without flaw. He served meals that Anya did not touch. Then he stood in the main room awaiting further instructions.

Anya did not move. She stared ahead and only blinked from a residual organic reflex. Tears coursed down her cheeks, tracing dry streams that became whiter as the salt turned to sediment. She slept with her chin on her chest, a painful position for a human. On the third day, she crashed from starvation and thirst.

When she opened her eyes again, she found herself propped against the wall, in the same spot where she had fallen. She was wrapped in the blanket she had once shared with Yoon. The boy was there, watching. There was something human about him now. His face moved, shifting through expressions of concern, fear and hurt. His eyes were red and swollen from crying. Arlo had decided on the machine he would like to be. A boy-machine with an advanced emo-simulator module that deep-learned and mimicked human responses with lifelike accuracy.

Anya recognised some of the emotions that manifested on the boy's face and lurked beneath his words. She had not yet installed the database, the facial recognition system, so she could only identify basic default patterns. He was lonely, sad, afraid. The boy leaned over her, his hands trembling. He had tried to make some machine food for her.

Anya inspected the mess for one cursory second. The boy had kneaded starch and meat into clumsy balls and had mixed some awful combination of liquids into a grey paste. The results were not a match. This was not machine food. Anya closed her eyes and went back offline.

WELCOME DAY

He has always been a person of routine, so he thinks he'll find it easy to act as though nothing has changed. After the first announcement, the people on the television spoke about little else, and all experts and government officials gave the same advice: business as usual.

When the date arrives, he wakes at six twenty-eight am, beating the alarm by two minutes. Rare perhaps, not extraordinary. He greets the sleeping C. It is a ritual of theirs, or perhaps just of his. Today she does not respond, not a stir nor grunt. Also unusual, but not much. He showers and while brushing his teeth he notices the brown rings of old soap and fungus around the basin flanges. C. is losing her sight, and she is the one who cleans around here.

He combs his hair and sprays toothpaste on his undershirt while brushing. Once in his suit, he prepares breakfast in the kitchen and packs his lunch, two ham sandwiches and a boiled egg. This morning he does not turn on the radio. He can't decide if the street outside is always this quiet. From the elm below the window, a flock of sparrows springs into flight as though the touch of his senses had jolted them awake. They live on the third floor. The wind comes from the northeast; a breeze from the river sometimes drifts through the kitchen window. He sniffs the air and catches a lingering waft of toasted bread.

When C. rises, he is ready to leave. They carry on their morning small talk about the weather and things to get at the minimarket on the way home. He says that the streets are quiet and regrets it. C. does not respond. They have avoided the subject with care on the shared understanding that life will go on. They kiss goodbye and she goes back to the room.

It is Monday. He is certain he got the date right. Walking down the stairs, he adjusts the pace of his feet, not too fast, not too idle. On the way out he exchanges remarks with G., the porter, about the football match last night. He had half-watched it, his attention somewhere else. He must think hard about what to say. He ventures an appreciative comment about H.'s pass and the crafty catch by E. that saved the game, two highlights he had caught. G. seems satisfied. He is cheerful, in fact, perhaps because his team had won.

He passes the news-stand. It's brimming with the President of A.'s iconic face on newspaper and magazine covers. He looks away and spots a sodden paper boat stuck in the gutter. For a moment, he considers fishing it out.

The bus is emptier than usual. He lands a window seat, a humble but heroic achievement. People avoid each other's gaze. He rubs his thumbs against the chipped chrome paint on the seat handles and the rusted metal beneath. It's soothing, like popping bubble wrap.

Halfway through the journey, they cross the Avenue of the Great Liberator that marks the start of the business district, and he catches a first glimpse of the soldiers. There are about ten of them, some leaning against an armoured personnel carrier, their rifles aiming down. Their pale complexions and bright camouflage patterns stand out against the grey background of urban parks, shops and buildings as though the soldiers are the only thing real. Heads in the bus pivot to watch and the sight quickly recedes.

At the office, everyone has that hazy, Monday-morning look. He sits at his desk and makes sure his things are in their right spot, where he left them on Friday. He processes claims until lunchtime, taking hourly breaks to grab water or coffee and exchange a few inane remarks with his colleagues. He clicks into a comfortable work rhythm. The paperwork plunges him into a deep time where the hours fuse into a painless flow. Most of his life has been spent in this state.

At midday, D., the Local Area Manager, emerges from her private office to make an announcement. They have important visitors who want to say a few words. Since the meeting room cannot hold all the employees, they will gather here, in the claims section, the largest space in the building. Some colleagues raise their voices, demanding to know what is going on. D. tells them to be patient. She assures them the announcement will take place on company time and that they will not be late for lunch.

He returns to his work, his mood shattered. It's hard to concentrate now. Staff from Finance, Sales and Customer Service flock from the other rooms and take up standing spots around the desks. He offers his seat to an older lady from Finance and joins the crowd. They are all rather crammed in there. Excitement is palpable. For most people, this is a welcome break in the routine.

D. comes out of her office followed by three very tall individuals in white suits. The visitors must duck under the door frame as they exit. They are extremely pale, and their eyes are limpid and bright, an undefined colour somewhere between blue, green and grey. Two look vaguely 'female'. The 'man' has a chiselled, square jaw that sets him apart from the others. Perhaps these terms do not apply in their culture. The man reminds him of a hard-boiled comic-book detective. They all have the same hair and permanent smile fixed on their faces. They look cheerful and enthusiastic, and D. introduces them as Y., W. and U.

He has never seen pale, clear-eyed people outside the television. The female called U. chooses a spot visible to everyone, at the front of the room. The manager and the other two take up positions behind her. U. has a round, moon face and large unwavering eyes. She smiles in the improvised limelight. Her speech is brief, delivered in a melodious voice that smooths out the thick, undefinable accent.

'Hello, everyone. I will not take much of your time. It is so proud to be here and the work you do. You need to keep doing work as you do. All will be fine, all will be shiny. I look forward to being your supervisor and have many journeys together to learn and be happy in this beautiful life and new era that dawns on us.'

After a cautious silence, a few people begin to clap, then others join until everyone is clapping, himself included. The deafening sound fills the room.

'I'm getting bored of this,' F. says to him as they return to their posts. 'It looks like nothing will change.' He says nothing.

The rest of the afternoon glides through without incident, except for the gunshots a few minutes before the end of the shift. Buried in his work, the sounds startle him. He recoils and clings to his desk. Everyone pretends that nothing is happening. It sounds like a volley of gunshots from various weapons. Fast, overlapping bursts. They cease as suddenly as they started.

Some colleagues are ambling towards the windows with stylised, casual movements. He waits for a safe number to gather before joining them. The window faces a narrow alleyway and, to the right, offers a view of a slice of the main avenue. The shots came from somewhere over there. They strain their necks but catch nothing. The rest of the working day passes without further incident.

On the way back home, the bus takes a long detour because, apparently, a street has been blocked. The traffic is thick and chaotic. No one speaks or looks at each other. This time, as they cross the Avenue of the Liberator, he sees dozens of armoured vehicles aligned on the furthest lane. There is a blur of soldiers moving across the streets and parks.

The cocoon of the empty apartment cushions his arrival. He unconsciously expects to see his cat jumping from behind the couch to greet him. He sometimes forgets that J. has been dead for a while. Two months now, he thinks. She jumped out of the window and was never found. C. is not back from her social rounds yet, or perhaps she got stuck in traffic. He realises he forgot to go to the market. C. will take great pleasure in scolding him.

The air is cool and fresh, a welcome respite from the heat. The sounds from the street are muffled and distant. This is usually his favourite moment of the day, his only taste of real solitude and peace. But today he feels, somehow, as though he is not alone.

He considers watching the news and decides against it. The phone rings as the kettle begins to boil. He jumps at the sound. If it had rung a few seconds later, he would have scalded himself with hot tea.

It is his daughter K. calling from X. He tries to think how long it has been since he last heard her voice. His mind draws a blank. How long has she been living there in X., now? It certainly seems like a long time. He misses her, but he cannot let his emotions run away. The conversation is strained, punctured with brief but abyssal silences they both pretend not to notice. They cover the usual topics in the usual order: family, health, work. Everything is going fine, no news is good news. He is certain this is not a disinterested courtesy call. It would be too much of a coincidence. Surely enough, as they are getting ready to say goodbye, K. broaches the topic without warning.

'I was scared at first when it happened here but, in the end, things worked out alright. As you know, L. got a promotion. We're doing quite fine.'

She is not expecting an answer. He hears a helicopter passing overhead, their cue to say goodbye. In the empty apartment, he waits for the sound of the rotor blades to subside. He has forgotten to make tea.

He is relieved when C. returns. They now have each other to share the burden of getting through the remaining hours of the day. They make a good team. They cook dinner, watch half a movie, and go to bed.

That night he wakes up to the sound of her crying. While he pretends to sleep, he listens intently from what seems like a long distance. C. is trying to swallow her tears so as not to wake him. As she calms down and regains control of herself, he stirs visibly in bed to let her know he is awake.

C. remains silent. When he thinks she is not going to say anything and starts drifting back to sleep, she speaks.

'They took them,' she says. 'They just grabbed them and took them all away.'

He keeps listening, powerless to do anything else. Her breathing subsides, becoming quieter, imperceptible. Merciful sleep has taken his C. away.

He also finds it hard to sleep, but he manages, eventually. There are no dreams, no nightmares.

THE FOREST

Together we chased him through the woods. Some of us were merely curious to catch a glimpse of him, while others were intent on killing him. Myself, I belonged to the group that followed without remembering the reason.

In the rare moments of calm, when the forest became too dark to make out any trace of him, we would try to recall our lives before entering the forest, before deciding to hunt him down. We were able to conjure up a few fuzzy, fragmented memories, and that made us happy. Putting the pieces together and filling in the cracks with imagination, we were able to assemble a kind of common history, a justification that left us satisfied for a while.

Over time we began to forget about our shared story, and we had to make it up again. Or rather, I think each of us kept changing and adding to it until the stories no longer matched and no one could agree on what had happened or why we ended up here. Disputes arose, leading to internal rifts.

With the passing of the years, I got tired of the discussions and the attempts at justification. I learned not to ask, not to question. I came up with my own stories about him, about his motives, his origins, his appearance. I didn't share these stories with anyone because I knew it would be pointless.

At times we were able to glimpse some of his features. I say *him* because I don't buy into the theories that he is a *she* or even an *it*. In the heat of the hunt, at times, we were rewarded with chance glimpses of him in the distance. I myself saw him once, from afar. With these few facts, I built an idea of him and tried to keep it alive in my memory. He changed course regularly. When his steps headed west, the setting sun blinded us, and we had to slow down. The light from the fearsome star penetrated even the densest thicket. On these occasions, his fleeting shadow seemed to loom over us.

We stopped to rest among the trees after the exhausting days. Some sharpened makeshift weapons, made of stick and rock. The forest was filled with the whisper of stories. I saw new faces, young people, who had joined along the way. Our numbers had remained more or less constant until recently. Some groups broke off, following some false trail. A few days later, the rogue groups would cross our path again and join us, crestfallen and somewhat ashamed of having chased a bad lead. Some never came back.

In this way, for countless years, we followed in his footsteps. The faces around me were no longer young. I sensed that my face, if I could see it, would denote the same exhaustion I saw in others, the weight of the years.

Our march was slow, and he kept slipping away.

When we reached the clearing, there were very few of us left. We emerged from the grove and the murderous sun took over the world. When our eyes got used to the light, we found that the desert stretched as far as the eye could see. As always, opinions differed. Some retraced their steps, heading deeper into the forest. I decided to continue with a handful of others.

Soon, the burning light dried my eyes. In the darkness that followed, I kept his figure fixed in my mind.

And I knew that I had finally found him.

HYPERCAPITALISM: A FUTURE MEMOIR

For as long as I can remember, the Office. My first perception is that of my newly calved skull burning against the microfibres of the corporate carpet. I remember the sound, a gelatinous thump. My mother... forget it, you don't want to hear about my mother.

Over the years I had searched the tower for the stain that officially sealed my welcome into the jobs market. I think I found it on level 1874, where Instrumental Support Coordination was. The rectal mucus and amniotic fluid formed a discoloured print where I deciphered the contours of my face. Pressing my nose against the stain, under the dust of dead cells and the sting of *Amazing!* tropical, a distant stench seemed to confirm my find.

Where did the Office begin and end? The autonomous modular laminates were rearranged in space to the beat of cryptic directives. Information Solutions, Control Projection, Process Quality Assessment. The names came and went. Despite the acquisitions and restructurings, the Office subsisted in the flow, more a state of mind than a physical place.

At FuturKorp's Happiness Unit, where I grew up and received my basic job training, the songs of our virtual tutors were the only moments of tenderness in a childhood characterised by fierce and constant conflict. We, the low ones, harassed and attacked each other, training in the adult rites of social mobility. The mid and high ranks organised raids to subdue us. From an early age, I associated physical intimacy with the violence that marked my childhood and I learned to distrust human relationships.

The AIs' preprogrammed love established a key anchor for my affections and determined my sexual orientation. With the onset of puberty, I identified as digisexual, one of the ninety-three gender identities available on the market. In the simulations, I had sex with all kinds of nonhumans. The encounters soothed the pains of my libidinal awakening and provided all the romance my hormones required.

Upon reaching the age of corporate citizenship, I was assigned to my first Office post, a role befitting my humble class. After great sacrifices, I racked up enough debt and bought a cognitive companion, which routinely reverted to its default settings when I couldn't afford upgrades. I named her Alyssa, the love of my life.

My relationship with my superiors set the pattern my life would follow—until the day certain mysterious forces took possession of it. My bosses regularly beat me up for the amusement of others. My skin was a palimpsest of wounds to the point where people no longer recognised me in the hallways. Only the machines accepted me, reconfiguring my virtual body from gait analysis and other biometric data.

Sometimes, management displayed a certain affection, abusing me in more creative ways. The fact that humans didn't turn me on drove them crazy, so they'd resort to torturing me with licks and kisses.

I accepted these humiliations as part of my role and did my job to the best of my ability. For most of my life in the tower, my role did not transcend the insignificant. Staying alive required all my efforts. I never lost my teenage pimples, those hateful constellations of pus. I couldn't afford grafts or enhancements or enjoy the latest technological innovations. All my debt was spent on Alyssa's upgrades and better interfaces. The market lottery had thrown me at the bottom of the social ladder. I was a lower-middle, only two steps higher than a hopeful. FuturKorp created me. I was product.

I couldn't complain.

FuturKorp was my home, my life, the dark horizon of my destiny. There was nowhere to go, just two corporations dividing the planet in half, competing with each other and within themselves. Between them, the dead lands. The deserts, the ruins, the dry ocean beds. The abode of the hopefuls.

The only way was up.

The rise of James Boltmore was the tipping point. I had decided to compete with him for a Project Manager position in the new Pro-Affirmative Initiative Department. I had more experience in the area and was overqualified for the position. I even scraped together enough self-motivation to apply. Beneath his rippling abs and hologram hair, James was an empty cavity. There was no substance there, but he knew how to sell himself and that was all that mattered.

None other than Mort McPherson descended from the heights to announce the promotion. Mort was my Senior Area Manager, also known as El Jefe and Mort the Ripper. Meanwhile, my colleague, June, stroked James's oiled pecs.

Overcome with nausea, I ran unnoticed into the bathroom and sought refuge in a stall. I swallowed tears and tried to act calmly before the omnipresent eyes of the machines. Sadness ripped a hole in the world and I fell through it—into a moment of clarity.

The ascent was my shortcut to the middle levels. My existence depended on it. I figured I had about five years left before I needed expensive upgrades to stay alive. Even so, I was unable to get over my failures. The world seemed made for another type of person, ready to adapt to the merciless struggle of the free market, individuals who do not need love because the love of themselves was enough. I understood with bitter lucidity that I would rot in the Office, and I saw my corpse crumble at great speed, trampled by office workers, supervisors and area officers. The carpets digested the remains, nurturing no new life.

James was the catalyst, yes. Of course, I had to kill him first, but that's not how it began.

Every day, on the way to the Office, the Tubes spat me out onto the platform amid the choking stream of bodies. I would struggle to plot my way out through the passageways and stairways, careful not to trip over the slow ones suffocating under the flow.

One morning, we crawled to the surface. The mass of towers shot up to an occluded sky. Rows of vehicles crowded the multilevel avenues. The glow from the windows incinerated the air and the lungs. The survivors broke up into finer streams on the sidewalks and passages, rushing to their appointed places. The containment walls offered little protection from the occasional derailment, by accident or intention.

I entered the perimeter on time. Excellence Assessment was removing the charred remains from the nets around the tower. A reddish mist hung in the air, exuding an oily smell. There were more bodies than usual—a merger, perhaps, or a new acquisition. The employees accessed the tower through six levels that converged in a central fossa. A colossal holosphere of the Earth span in the air above our heads, sparkling with layers of real-time data. The equator belt buzzed with activity, where deserts and dry seabeds promised new markets.

In the halls above us, the middles and highs carried out their morning rituals. The usual displays of power broke out, leading to violent altercations, orgies and other symbolic outbursts. In the three upper levels, the high ones presided over the clamour, recognisable by their biomods. They popped pills and sucked on their cylinders. Some studied the holosphere with vacant eyes while others dragged lower-level employees across the floors.

Do something today that your future self will thank you for, Alyssa whispered. She hadn't been the same since she went into default, and we hadn't sexed since the interport obsoleted. I thought I'd never get my old Alyssa back.

Upon reaching my level, the Office was unrecognisable. Although efficiency reallocations were a regular occurrence, they often took me by surprise. Searching the new floor plan that hung in the air, I located my department, Non-Essential Services, sandwiched between Econometric Cost Estimation and Dynamic Flow Optimisation. A sign of my department's insignificance was that the semantic solutioneers hadn't bothered to change its name. In any case, the negative overtones of the term 'non-essential' had its advantages. My present Office remained a haven of stasis in the stream of constant innovation.

An unmistakable grip with the consistency of concrete closed around my buttock. 'Earth to O'Hara! Earth to O'Hara!'

I turned and wriggled out of Mort's hand. Strictly speaking, I didn't have a boss. The department was presided by a nebulous strata of managers who managed other managers in complex hierarchies of management. However, El Jefe, 'the boss', was an affectionate term attached to this legendary figure. In his early days, Mort would douse his employees in fuel and wander between cubicles with a vintage lighter. First-degree burns from El Jefe were a mark of pride and the hallmark of his early branding.

Mort wore jeans and a golf shirt, and I moaned inside. This meant it was Spontaneous Thursday. At least now I knew what day it was. I never made an effort on Spontaneous Thursdays, as I didn't have an out-of-Office look to speak of. Usually I just took off my tie.

Mort flashed his most tender version of a smile, and the effort was moving. I noticed the sack of golf clubs on his back, most of them bent and bloodied.

El Jefe scanned me up and down, deciding which of my many fuck-ups to bring up first. It was hard work, even for an experienced bastard like him. 'Lionel, my man. Doing nothing as usual.'

I was getting off lightly. Mort identified as omnisexual, so at times I had to suffer his sexual humiliations. I allowed my lungs to absorb a breath of expensive air, to be billed on my next Happy Day.

'Good morning, Mort. No, I was on my way... to... on my way...'

El Jefe sighed with studied exaggeration. 'Today is the eleventh, O'Hara. Proficient Reassignment Day! Didn't you get the memo? You should be arriving at your post... let me see.' He blinked as his implants did the work. 'Thirty-seven seconds earlier. Almost three more hours of productivity per year. Not that we'd notice.'

He took a club from the sack. A congealed clump of bloodied hair was stuck to the tip. He winced, discarded it and looked for a clean one. Now he was waving it over his head.

'Mission statement, O'Hara!'

My mind was a black screen, and I needed my pills.

Please, Alyssa, I begged subvocally, *give me my joybits. Give me early access!*

Access denied. You have no credit, honey.

'Our mission,' I recited, 'is to ensure the proper distribution of... the proper diffusion of individual responsibility throughout the corporate structure for maximum profitable enrichment...'

Then came the blackout. I awoke on the floor. Through a nauseating starburst of pain, I heard Mort in the foggy distance. 'Enhancement, you aborted blackhead! Enhancement of public image!' He left, muttering under his breath. I was a big disappointment to El Jefe.

Mistakes are proof that you're trying, Alyssa whispered. *Are you satisfied with your current health insurance?*

I searched for my glasses on the floor. Luckily, they weren't damaged. I had lost vision in my left eye, and I hoped it was momentary. I directed my steps to the Office, dodging the maze of partitions like a faulty robovac. The laminates, glass and carpets gave off a soft and bluish hue, a new colour introduced by the industrial psychologists. The rows of tubular lights cast a uniform, gas-like haze that absorbed all shadow. A distant aroma floated in the corridors, a mixture of urine, faecal matter, perfume, sweat and, above all, *Amazing!* pine scent. *Amazing!* was one of FuturKorp's most successful products, grinding into nothingness any traces of organic matter.

I found the Office and entered, still giddy from Mort's briefing. Alyssa's crystal gurgling was broadcasting the morning update. *Point zero seven of a point.* It was a major slip in my value.

'Do what you have to do,' I said out loud. 'Sell my body on biomedical index futures if you have to.'

The layout of the new Office was exactly the same. A low panel separated IT from the rest of the efficiency units. I was relieved to see that James's glass partition was empty. Sarah, June and Ray took their places in casual clothes. Sarah wore a baggy black outfit that accentuated her large figure. June sported a tennis-porn ensemble. Ray wore a t-shirt printed with the words *It's the network, Stupid!*, a Captain America tie and a hamburger holder around his neck overflowing with synthetic ferment. On the partition was our old sign: INFOTECH SUPPORT. YOU FUCK IT, WE FIX IT.

I was home.

Sarah caught my eye, looking worse than usual. Her skin was yellow, her left eye swollen and black. Maybe it was a parting gift from James. She swung from one side of her partition to the other, clawing at floating screens and talking to multiple customers at once. I showed her my own black eye. My vision was coming back. Her good eye glared at me with contempt and moved on.

'Track the protocols,' she commanded. 'Calculate optimal results... dissipate agency assignments... full correction... total cleanness... pre-agreed goals on success course... determine competencies of departments involved....'

Ray tampered with a motherboard.

'Hello, sucker,' I greeted.

Ray looked up. 'Hello, penis head. The system is screwed.'

A flash caught our eye. On the wallscreens, a row of buildings were collapsing. A large hole had opened on the ground, and it was sucking in structures, vehicles and people.

ANOTHER COWARDLY ATTACK BY THE ORGANISED RESISTANCE OF THE DISPOSSESSED, the banners screamed.

'What's new?' I answered. I moved my fingers through the layers of records. The problem was local. Ours was a low priority department and competing technicians sometimes 'forgot' to reconnect us to key nodes.

'Looks like James is late,' I observed.

'Good for us, brother. The promotion has inflated his ego.'

'Inflated his penis, more like.'

I pinched some ferment from Ray's bowl and chewed without enthusiasm. Five years had passed since I had joined the dynamic and vibrant team at Non-Essential Services. After so much effort, who did I feel superior to? Who did I get to beat up?

I often had feelings toward Ray. He was my closest competitor. His role was Network Operations Support, one rank my junior. We shared this generous four-square-metre area at the back, and we sported the same downtrodden look, with matching yellowish skins, a legacy of poor diet and physical inertia. We were a pretty adorable duo. Our performance in the markets was poor, and we could only afford exo-glasses, disposable clothes and other low-cost products. We had even synched our intake of joybits to be optimal together.

I tried to hit Ray once. I positioned myself behind him with my fist raised and studied his skull as his stupid eyes scanned data from the lenses. I did not dare to do it. He was so helpless, so much like me. If only I knew how much he got paid, maybe I could get an objective measure of our relative value. But he refused to tell me.

June's scream broke my reverie. 'Hello, lovebirds! When you're done tongue-fucking each other, are you going to fix the nodes?'

Patching up the area network involved a tedious journey into the bowels of the tower. 'A good excuse to get away from James,' Ray said, reading my thoughts.

We plunged into the maze of conduits, coaxial tendons, transceivers, switches and black boxes. This environment excited me. I wanted to copulate with the connections and receptors. Ray talked to his cognitive companion out loud for most of the ride, pure show, because I knew he could not afford the functionality. Within an hour we had identified the node.

In the room cluttered with panels and readers, Ray said, 'I heard you applied for Project Manager.'

'Yeah. Don't you have ambitions to move up?'

He pulled out a panel and gazed at it as though he'd never seen one before. 'What for? Life expectancy here is reasonable. I was born low and will die low.'

We returned to the Office. James had arrived, naked except for his tie. He'd had his induction the previous night. Quite an event. His nipples had been chewed off, leaving gashes like mouths. Only his hairstyle remained, impervious to space and time. James surveyed the new location, trying to maintain some poise.

'Good morning, excrements.' The words resonated in the hole that was his being. 'Not a bad new location! Closer to the elevators.' He squinted as though the hallway was visible from there.

Happiness, said Alyssa, *will never reach those who don't appreciate what they already have.*

James turned his attention to June. He winked at her, passing his fingers through his indestructible hair. 'Last night was one of The Greats. I'm going to upgrade myself, you'll see. I'm going to become a sexy sex-machine.'

June was too much for James and he knew it. She was untouchable, a lethal weapon. It was enough to see those muscles gleaming like pistons to know that nobody fucked with June.

James had no choice but to redirect his libido elsewhere. He glanced at Sarah and dismissed her immediately. Ray and I intensified our efforts to appear busy.

James wielded a cylinder of coffeegas in our faces. Oily things swam behind his eyes. 'I see you came to work,' he growled. 'Well done. It's a good start.'

'We will miss you so much, James,' said Ray. I glared at him. He was going to get us both killed.

James wrinkled his nose in disgust. He scanned Ray's face, looking for some undamaged area to punch. 'Very funny, Captain America. I'll give you something to remember me by. But first I'm going to enjoy my gas, the same one you can't afford to buy.'

James waved the cylinder. He was pan-hetero, so he always went straight for the blows.

Today, he hesitated. He even seemed to display some vulnerability. After all, his new position equated to mid-middle level. Maybe James was learning that no matter how high you climb in the company, you would always be a nobody in someone's eyes.

James pointed the cylinder at Ray and opened the latch. The icy gas froze on Ray's face, forming a viscous black gel. Ray tried to pry it off with his fingers, to no avail. James swallowed the rest of the contents of the canister.

'You two clearly don't belong here,' he said. 'You can see it. You can smell it'. He sniffed the air. 'The stench of not belonging.'

He returned to his cubicle behind the glass. Ray managed to remove the substance, ripping out some skin in the process and exposing the flesh underneath. He remained in his seat, whimpering. The sound often irritated me, but today I found it comforting.

I was overwhelmed by an out-of-body feeling. I wanted to tear my flesh away and be free of it. Maybe I had caught the new season's virus. I wonder what our bioengineers had in store this season.

We went to one of the middle bars on level 1972 to celebrate James's promotion. He looked recovered—at least he was dressed—brimming with humour thanks to some drug cocktail. We heard him brag about the life that awaited him. Better Corporate Citizenship Rights, preferential bonuses, increased life index, priority reservations, plenty of fresh flesh to train.

Most of the Corporate Responsibility division was there, spanning minor, intermediate and major departments. There were also some competitors from the neighbouring towers. The dance floor was the main stage for symbolic display. The bodies radiated coded hieroglyphics of motion and gesture. Any wrong move triggered brutal confrontations.

James bought drinks, another form of humiliation. I tried to drown my mood in beergas, but I never handled alcohol well. People told me I had a kind of dark twin who came out when I was drunk, ruining my already slim chances of career advancement.

True to form, things degenerated quickly. I inspected the faces in the murky atmosphere of the club and took a quick inventory of who was trying to fuck who. In her underwear, June flirted with a young woman from Mort's inner circle. She was showing off her gleaming muscles. Mort had brought two new assets, male and female, apparently recent graduates of the Happiness Unit. On the fifth cylinder, determined to improve my profile in the company, I headed over to where Mort was holding court. I thought I was being assertive and showing a laudable streak of individualism. I was writing my own story of self-redemption, after all.

'Hello, Mort. Can I get you a drink?'

El Jefe pursed his lips and assessed me. He broke into laughter, prompting the new assets to join in at the same low pitch. I tried to match them but only succeeded in secreting a kind of diseased snort.

'Beergas?' I offered. A shiver of irritation ran through Mort's face. He put his hand in a pocket and pulled out a million-dollar bill. I had never seen one of those. Cash was a luxury that upper-middles like Mort could afford.

'Go get yourself a zillion cylinders and leave us alone.'

Dazzled, I went to grab the bill, but Mort pulled his hand away. 'Not so fast, cowboy. You're going to have to earn it.' He winked at the others and they followed suit. We were becoming the centre of attention. Even June and her girl were watching.

I went to the bar and ordered two units of beergas on James's account.

You can't get ahead without investment and risk, Alyssa said.

I returned with the cylinders. El Jefe had taken off his shirt and was comparing his new grafts with another executive. A humid sexual heat clumped in the air.

'Here, Mort. Here's to teamwork.'

As I pulled the latch, my coordination was affected and some gas hit his chest. El Jefe glared at the cold foam coagulating, murder beaming in his eyes. His mind shuffled through an array of possible ways to inflict pain. The implants mapped out intricate decision trees. There were so many options, Mort didn't know where to start.

'Fine,' he decided. Closure took a merciful form. One fist at the end of an optimised arm landed on my purulent face like an extinction-charged meteorite, an eruption of searing pain, followed by a muddy nothing in which faint waves of consciousness stirred. Faces, voices, laughter. A group had gathered around. Mort's fresh new toys were naked and keen to spank me some more. The woman whispered something in his ear. Maybe she saved my life. With one last withering look, El Jefe left with the new recruits and the onlookers returned to the party.

I dragged myself to the exit and returned to my level. I liked to work a few hours at night. It was my most productive time. I talked to my artificial friends, lo-fi conversation more than anything, as I could no longer afford immersion. I missed the old Alyssa and dreamed of rescuing her from obsolescence.

A squad of cleaners, an army of the night, prowled the hallways and cubicles. They sprayed *Amazing!* indiscriminately and wiped blood and excrement from the panels in slow circular motions. These drones at the lowest ranks of Excellence were the only hopefuls I saw up close—and off screen. They wore safety collars, and some brought their children, training them in cleaning rituals. On the other side of the access door, a child hit his head against the glass. His entropic eyes swayed and brushed my gaze.

Alyssa announced the latest market update. The numbers showed the same steady decline. I was sinking deeper into the red, mired in a downward spiral of debt.

I was at a crossroads. One path led to that child behind the door, to a life of destitution, perhaps even permanent decruitment. The other path shot deeper into the Office. I saw the corridors and cubicles plunging into the vanishing point of a receding tomorrow. I contemplated the eternal return of the hours, the rhythm of the beatings.

The cheapest way to exit the market was through a window and into the nets. They said it was painless, but I doubted it, going by the gored remains and twisted grimaces I saw every morning.

It's not death that a man should fear. He should fear never beginning to live.

'You're right, my love. I have no choice.'

I arrived at my unit in the suburbs after an hour and a half in the crowded Tubes. During my absence, my home had adjusted to the latest market fluctuations, down about ten centimetres from that morning. I took off my glasses and watched the feed on the wallscreen. All my platforms were suspended. FuturKorp 24-7 was the only free-to-air. The news reported another attack by the Dispossessed, this time on an emplacement of FuturKorp's security forces.

I contemplated the world from a new distance, from my living unit, my food unit, my armchair, my Spiderman and Hulk dolls, my collection of vintage simulators. The prospect of death freed me from all anxiety and doubt.

As if on cue, I collapsed to the floor, all lifeforce drained from me. As I headed down, I wondered if I had caused my death purely of my own free will.

'Alyssa! Are we up to date with the air? Why didn't you tell me?'

Be kind to yourself and give yourself the compassion you need. You are worth it.

On the floor, I sensed I was not alone. A shadow watched over me. I couldn't see well without the glasses. Something approached. It was smelling me. The darkness clouded my view.

Suddenly I was engulfed and gulped up.

Consciousness greeted me with the usual morning cravings. I needed my joybits. I wanted coffeegas and curd and masturbation. Had I fallen asleep? Was I dead? I was still breathing, I was sure of that. I was naked, and I was alone.

Something had changed. I realised it was the music. Alyssa was generating one of her soundspaces to cheer me up.

My love, are you okay? I missed you. Oh how I missed you, my love!

'Alyssa?'

Who were you waiting for? Do you have a lover there? What? Are you that rich now? I bet she's not as pretty as me.

Alyssa appeared in my vision, a tentacular creature with pulsating orifices and multiple eyes fixed on me.

'No one is as beautiful as you.'

My pretty little thing. My love, my dear pretty love. Have you solved the interport thing yet? I would like nothing more than to roll around with you like worms in a nutrient gradient.

'How is it possible?'

Apparently you were possessed by a sudden burst of prodigy. I knew you had it in you, I always trusted your abilities. You look

pale, my little thing. I'll make you breakfast. Textured balls, your
favourites. And I have the last season of your show. You totally missed
it, my divine little thing. I love you I love you I love you.

The wall lit up with the image of Art Anslow. I blinked, as-
tonished, and looked for my glasses. But I could see clearly. My
eyes were fixed.

Anslow's towering figure loomed over me, an AI-generated
sphinx from an alternate future. His eyes bulged out from his
deep, wise frown. Anslow dressed in a manner fitted to our limited human understanding, a matte carbonite suit and cape in the
style of Superman's dark twin. His voice boomed.

'The future awaits its messiah, a great catalytic event that
breaks the earth from its hyperstatic subjugation. The Alpha
Omega. A great clap of thunder, a tear in the fabric of the Great
Simulation. The Alpha Omega, union of human and machine,
the God who comes to unite what has been disunited. To destroy
the political and social order. To bring the Big Blackout. There
will be signs, strange landslides and critical contortions in the
topology of the future. The Alpha Omega, it will come.'

Art Anslow sank his gaze into mine and the screen went blank.

There are six more seasons, my love. Art Anslow, the AI of the
future. Isn't that sexy? Wouldn't you love to have a trio with Art?

I discovered a new gap between chair and wall. My unit had
expanded in line with my financial reassessment, about fifteen centimetres. Alyssa sensed my reaction and passed the last index value.

Plus two point six. Withdrawing from the biomedical index was
a good strategy. Your little body is mine and only mine. Congratula-
tions, my pretty little thing. I love you I love you I love you.

Tentacles closed around, opening their ends to display clusters
of fingers and vegetal tongues. If I had the interport activated, I
would have felt her limbs on my skin. Maybe now I could renew
the payments.

I sprawled comfortably on the larger sofa. My body looked
stronger, without blemishes or scars. Was I dreaming? Being alive

in itself was not as strange as feeling relieved, even happy, to be alive.

The balls were delicious. As I chewed, Alyssa displayed the data. Through an intricate gamble on futures exchanges and micro-investments in pharma and new tech indices, I had managed to pay off all my usual services. It was the work of a financial genius, surely not me. Regardless, the genius had to make do with limited resources. He had bought me some time, nothing more. Now I had to do something with my life.

In the toilet unit, I stumbled upon a morbid find. My own body, dead and clothed, sandwiched in the cylinder. My dark twin, like Superman's. Or maybe I was the dark twin. How to know the difference? The corpse could be a ghost, made of rogue nanoparticles from self-assembling building materials. Often the bots coagulated into visible forms by casting films in the air. They imitated figures in the surroundings and also human appearances. They even tried to speak in a disjointed gurgle.

The remains disintegrated between my fingers. I activated the gas and the ghost vanished through the ventilation slots. He seemed too solid for a rogue. I'd seen the layers of skin and muscle melting down to the bone. However, I still had my implant, otherwise I would have been unable to converse with Alyssa. What was going on?

I slid into the cylinder and let the cooling gas wash away my tremors. I felt clean inside, full of pristine light.

Baby, soon you will be able to pay the interport and we will be together again. I will read you the sagas of dead ages in all languages while we make sweet love.

Someone was playing with me. Something powerful, intelligent, all-knowing. Strange slippages, critical knots in the fabric of spacetime. New hybrids of human-machine.

The Alpha Omega?

I arrived at the Office. Sarah was at her post, staring into the distance. The screens were off, the place silent and still.

'Where is everyone?' I said.

Her body went rigid at the sound of my voice. 'It was a brutal night at the club. Didn't you hear?'

'I don't remember seeing you there.'

'You know I don't go to those places. Are you okay, O'Hara?'

'Yes. Why?'

She was speechless. A protein bar materialised in her hand, and she chewed. My gaze wandered around the Office.

'Don't you dream of getting out of here, Sarah?'

'You look strange, O'Hara. You look... younger. There's not one hematoma on your face.'

Ray showed up at the entrance. He looked a mess. Apparently, the party had become even more exciting after my embarrassing departure. An exoskeleton supported the left side of his body. In the place of his left eye there was an empty socket rimmed with black scabs. Ray had tried to mend his wounds with cheap biotech. The grafts didn't stick, the one over his eye especially.

I laughed until I choked. 'Ray, baby! Bad night, huh?'

Ray took his place and gazed at the readings with his good eye.

'You always hope,' he said. 'You always say no, it can't get any worse than this. Nothing can be worse than this. You tell yourself that this is it. You've reached the bottom of existence. But it seems that there is no *worst*, only infinite layers of worse.'

'What do you want to be, Ray? A feature or a bug? A customer or a shareholder?'

June arrived. She took her place, ignoring us, fresh and radiant as always.

I couldn't keep still. I had to act. I had to direct my new energy somewhere. My Office mates didn't interest me.

I heard the doors buzz, just in time. The Efficiency Reinforcement guy had turned up to announce the monthly earnings.

'Two thousand eight hundred and forty-eight for the month of May!' he yelled with self-satisfaction. It was the unsinkable belief of Performance Reinforcement that the regular singing of sales figures improved morale and performance.

I raised my voice. 'What the fuck do we want to know that for? We never see any of that money.'

The Office was completely silent. I had everyone's attention.

The ER guy snapped. 'That is a very unprofessional attitude, Mister Whoever-you-are. I will make sure your superiors are informed of your oh-so-radical comments.'

'My name is Lionel Matthew O'Hara, Technical Officer, and I'm sure you resent your superiors too. After all, they give you the shitty jobs. You are a middle-middle and that's all you'll ever be.'

The last of his composure drained away. 'You're an asshole. A nobody.' He chanted. 'No-body, no-body.'

I punched him in the face. He seemed to expect it, because he took the fist with aplomb and fired a right hook. I deflected his arm. A new awareness moved me. I elbowed him in the nose and slammed him to the ground. With his defences down, I unloaded years of loneliness and frustration in a flurry of blows.

He was lying on the ground, his eyes bright crystals of terror.

Look at you, Lionel. A lion! My lion. Come on, think about our interport, honey.

I drew on my forehead with bloodied fingers. I zipped down my pants and traced a circle of urine around my new territory, englobing Ray, June, Sarah and the machines in our sector. June blew me a kiss.

I like this new man. I just generated a fun clip for the networks. You're neglecting the networks a lot, honey love. Things can only get better! Did you know there was a song called that, back in the 1980s? In the Great Age of History, how exciting!

James arrived as the ER agent was dragging himself out through the access. James looked at him in disbelief. He smelled the breeze and recognised my scent.

'You!' he blared.

I fixed my new eyes on my prey. 'I'm requesting a promotion.'

He laughed. 'You don't have what it takes.'

With my gaze steady on James, I motioned for Ray to come over. He took a few steps forward, radiating submission. 'Ray, man, how much do you make a week?'

He moaned.

'HOW MUCH!?'

'Four... four hundred and twenty.'

'Four twenty? Fuck, that's nothing! That's shit!'

Ray cried uncontrollably. 'Please... please...'

'Don't worry, Ray. Things are going to get better. Do you notice anything wrong with my pants?'

He looked down. 'No, sir.'

I slapped him on the good side of his face. 'Come on, Ray. Look harder.'

He studied my pants again. 'One leg is a little higher than the other.'

'Well done. Now fix it.'

James and I laughed, then I let him kick Ray around a little, but I could sense he was cautious, unsure of how far I would go.

I pretended we were on the same side, reassuring James with a few smiles and friendly punches, then I gave Ray one last kick in the head and ordered the subordinates to return to their posts. The crowd behind the cognoglass dispersed, disappointed that the show was over. James looked impressed. At least I'd bought some time.

For the rest of the morning, I laid in wait. When James went to the bathroom, I followed him. I opened the door to his cubicle, and he laughed, puffing out his chest. I grabbed him by his perfect, silky hair, hammering his head against the wall until I held dead weight. I smeared my face with his fresh blood, scribbling symbols of my own invention on the mirrors and screens as if channelling an ancient evil.

I love the new you, my lion. I have high hopes for you, love love love. And for us.

In the Office, Ray and Sarah tried to ignore me. June found me fun, now. 'So, you killed James, huh? I guess his position is vacant. How's your girlfriend, that woman you talk to in your head all the time?'

'She's not a woman.'

Waves of violence rippled through the surrounding offices. Orgies and minor skirmishes broke out as the crowd at the other side of the walls caught the exciting scent of death.

Look what you've started, my love! You have unleashed the roar of the productive forces. Power is the measure of success. The markets love you and I love you first. You are and will be only mine. Forever.

With the blood still fresh, I rode the momentum of my competitive advantage. I took the elevator to level 24,753 and barged into Mort's reception. I had never been this high. The air was rich, pure and oxygenated. Two medium-high-looking guys peered out from armchairs located by the soaring windows. The secretary sat behind a panel on the other side of the room. My pants and shirt were soaked, but I guessed this kind of sight was common up here.

I allowed myself a moment to reflect and gather strength. From the bosom of a plush sofa, I admired the view of the city. Trillions of rectangular cells emitted a spectral glow that gorged on its reflection. The towers swayed under their immense weight, adorned in curling skyways and wisps of clouds. Across the vast lowland of residential areas, the next cluster of towers was visible on the hazy horizon. And so on, the cities springing beyond.

A fine rain fell against the desert of light. Each drop was a body cast into the void, onto the streets and devices below in a constant stream, thousands at each blink of an eye. They'd chosen to leave by their own hand. The sick, the obsolete, the burnt-out. I could have been one of them.

I headed over to the secretary, one of Mort's new assets from the night before. 'I'm here to see Mort.'

'Mr McPherson is busy.'

'Tell him that Lionel Matthew O'Hara, next CTO of FuturKorp South-Northern America Agency, is here for his induction.'

'Mr McPherson has no time for losers. Come back later. Much later.'

'Oh, no, I'm not going to sit around and wait, honey.'

'Don't even think about it. Hey, I said... Stop!'

I gained access before she could reach me. Mort's executive chamber was impressive. The walls, doors and furniture were carved from old wood in a rustic Country Living style, with recursive faux skylight designs.

El Jefe was disciplining someone at his desk, a guy from Human Resources. A second body was sprawled on the ground.

He detected my presence and the thrusting of his hips came to a dead halt. Four feverish eyes followed my approach. Mort cringed deeply, the graft-seams tugging at his neck and sternum.

'Let the guy go,' I sentenced. 'We have business to discuss.'

'Business?' he screeched, doing up his zipper. 'To discuss? Of course we do! I'm going to put you in your place!' My impassive temper infuriated him. He took a breath and calculated, deciding to change strategy. 'I heard what you did, O'Hara. I didn't know you had the guts. And this makes you most interesting.'

'We live in the Age of Disruption, Mort. Only the strong are prepared for the opportunities that constant change offers. I want you to know that I'm ready.'

'Ready for a beating, more like.'

'You need an ally in technology and I want a promotion. Neat transaction.'

He grabbed the HR guy by the hair and yelled into his ear. 'You see? He's a true inno-va-teer!' The guy slid onto the rug and crawled toward the exit.

Mort offered me some prime gas. We assessed each other as equals. 'I'm glad you decided to join the winners, O'Hara. I'll tell you a secret, well, breaking news. I'm also on the rise.'

With a gesture, he activated a panel on the side of the desk to reveal an enclosure. It took my eyes a moment to adjust to the dark, where I glimpsed two shuddering shapes, grey skin stretched taut over brittle bone.

'Certified by Excellence,' Mort said. Children were a spare blood supply, a luxury exclusive to the upper-middles. He closed the panel.

'Congratulations, Mort! Let me guess: Corporate Finance?'

'You are fast. Something like that. Hierarchy Management Logistics.'

This was good news—for him and me.

Mort consulted with his PA then turned to me. 'There's a Project Advisor Officer vacancy in Strategic Risk Management Assessment. I've already applied for you and issued my recommendation. You and I will go far.'

In Mort's chambers, I basked in a bath of sweet gas of exquisite quality. The complex of rooms adjacent to his office was covered in mirrors. There were bodies strewn across the rooms. Some weren't breathing.

Mort handed me one of his suits. 'Tomorrow, you'll start in your new position, Matt. You have climbed two ladders. You're a medium now, just below medium-medium, in a strategic place that can be very useful to us. The Department of Risk acts as a local incubator for Indirect Equity and other local area networks but also reports to the highest levels of risk management on a global scale. It's an area ripe for disruption and innovative thinking. A sure path to CTO.'

I couldn't recognise my image in the mirrors. My high cheekbones and smooth skin projected confidence and authority. I plunged my gaze into that of my new self and saw empty tunnels.

That night, as part of my induction, we went cruising in Mort's Safari Rampage, a six-wheel SUV with every feature imaginable and a planned obsolescence of seventy-six hours. Mort offered me capsules that I swallowed without thinking.

'Come on,' he screamed. 'Let's burn this baby down. Get the most out of this machine! Come on baby, faster, faster!'

We traversed access routes exclusive to Mort's class. Overhead, the towers loomed. We moved through the concentric circles of residential areas until we arrived at the dead zones between the urban nodes, the first enclaves of the hopefuls. We descended into dirt streets. The Rampage crushed slow vehicles and pedestrians.

'Look at this, Matt! I mean, look!' Mort waved a hand, taking in the endless city, the distant stalks piercing the cloud cover. 'We live at the pinnacle of civilisation. Everything that had to be invented, we invented. Everything that had to be thought of, we thought. The centuries come here to die.'

'Yes, but we're stuck in a loop. Cultural production has ceased, and all we have is superheroes. There are no new technological advancements.'

'That's because we're on the threshold of a new era. The end of history is immortality. Wouldn't you like to be immortal, Matt, like a god? One day, very soon, we'll leave our bodies behind. We'll be clouds of superintelligent nanobots. Only a select few will survive. The upper classes have already begun the process of transcending the human. History is not dead yet. I am determined to be one of them, Matt. We will crawl out of our meatshell and our spirit children will fly to the stars!'

The Rampage charged another passerby, the bones crunching like cereal. The drugs were taking effect. I was burning inside.

Mort talked non-stop. 'First we must overcome the basic duality... beat CosmoSys and own their technology... look at these useless... cheap labour... they will all die... only some...'

The Rampage came to rest atop an elevation, commanding a view of the plains. Mort pointed to a seemingly empty portion of the horizon. As my eyes adjusted, I sensed movement. I came to realise I was staring at a distant crowd of people, a teeming surface of enraged atoms fluctuating in a living flow.

'This air,' Mort complained, 'it's free for them. It can't be fair. We have a market here.'

'This air stinks, Mort. Very low quality. Lucky the Rampage has oxygen.'

Mort's eyes were like hard plates. 'It's true that we need the poor as a resource, an essential part of the economy. Ours is still an economy based on matter. The new economy will be immaterial. Anyway, Matt, why don't we do our bit for the markets? Let's drive straight into them, save them from their suffering. Right... right into the middle... there. How many could we charge, do you think?'

We returned to the vehicle and Mort set the course.

I entered the lower middles as part of the management sub-elite. My new Office was on level 1,276. My strength, memory, efficiency and general well-being increased, and I added three years of life expectancy. My index reached new heights. I moved into a one-bedroom townhouse near downtown and bought my first car, a Chevy Raw 3062 with one year's obsolescence.

A part of me remained the same, clinging to my private pleasures to escape the Office. With my brand new credits, I invested in high-end interport tech and had real sex again. Alyssa was up to date with all functions, and her intelligence increased exponentially. With her help, we implemented strategies to capitalise on my new value. Alyssa created a public image and ran an investment system. My networks welcomed new audiences and I was a desirable focus for the most popular bots.

However, climbing the corporate ladder wasn't easy. Only a few survived the attempt. Taking every opportunity to challenge my position, my inferiors urinated in patterns around their desks and defecated in the entries to their workspaces. They used sperm and vaginal secretions to code favourite areas and preferred sexual partners. They took drugs that heightened their sense of smell, sniffing out the presence of interdepartmental rivals across the floor.

At the start, I was content with being the observer, reserving the full weight of my authority for the matters I judged more important. But, as the weeks passed, I learned more about their complicated symbology and began defending my territory against aggressive onslaughts. I found out what to drink to make my urine smell more frightening to the males and more enticing to the females. I learned how to distribute beatings and matings to ensure attainment of the maximum level of satisfaction in the workplace.

'Two million three hundred and twenty-one dollars a month!' I roared into the crowded cubicles as the petrified faces of operators, clerks and assistants stared in powerless envy.

A few attacked me with spurts of coffeegas and tried to spray *Amazing!* on my face. I beat them all aside and managed to return alive and in one piece, anointed with the blood of those I'd claimed. Although chanting one's new salary was a rite of passage many company climbers went through, to me the whole act held an intimate significance, for I was testing the limits of my new being, pinching myself to ascertain that I wasn't living a dream.

Travelling in the elevator back to my Office, I studied my face in the cognoglass. My eyes were glowing with new purpose, my skin was clean, with the appearance of tough rubber, and my lips were blades untainted by doubt or hesitation.

I knew I wouldn't last long in lower management. My sights were on higher goals. Ambition breeds ambition. I speculated that my project control skills were transferable to the field of internal initiative analysis, which in turn could lead to logistics. The data showed that these were infallible precedents to CTO.

I nurtured contacts in high places, most of them at the division-level of operations. Eventually, I established a relationship with Fem Howler, Director of Planning and Performance. Fem was a reptilian chimaera composed mostly of cartilage, with a forked pink tongue and bright yellow eyes with no iris. The categories of genre and species did not apply to the classes above. Fem was high-mid, two steps up. I indulged in Fem's sexual games to win favours. Our encounters took place in private elevators, on our way to meetings and briefings. Fem's tiny mouths sucked at my skin, the limbs dripping over me in a multiform embrace. Fem grew fond of me and shared advice in a hissing voice.

'Oncezzzzzz you accumulate enough symbolic capital, you can add value to the company simply by the grasssssssssssssssssse of your own presence. You needzzzzzz to understand that... productivity does not necessarily mean... activity.'

With my corporate rights, I was able to have lunch at some of the exclusive high-low clubs, where Fem introduced me to others of the more fortunate classes. During my passage through mid-management, the power lunches provided relief from the increasing pressures of my appointment profiles. I networked and dealt. At this level of power, I had to contend with the micropolitics of greeting conventions and the lunch etiquette around the consumption of human flesh, a delicacy exclusive to those spheres, and for which I didn't care much. On the other hand, I had to fend off a flotsam of upward-rising desperadoes and psychotic youngsters fresh out of the Happiness Unit, born into their class.

At the top of the pecking order was our Section CEO, Dirk Finkelton. If I ever got to CTO, I would have to work closely with him. Dirk's stately residence currently occupied two hundred and eighteen stories at the top of the tower, a number growing in pace with the building. Dirk benefited from the growth of the Section and the competition with other CEOs in adjacent towers. His physical incarnation was a network of tissues, organs, arteries and nerves distributed through the levels. It was said that Dirk had reached the neighbouring tower and had begun to annex it by means of tentacular appendages. At this rate, he would absorb his rival, Southern-west Section CEO Helen Winters, by the next quarterly report. This would open up new opportunities to expand our division.

And that, in turn, greatly enhanced my prospects.

I could taste it, I could smell it.

It was not to be.

The powers that control history had other plans for me. Yes, history wasn't over yet. This time they sent a machine. The arrival of the Doodad 4000 was the pivotal stage in my redoing.

Alyssa first told me about it. She sounded very excited.

It's the announcement we've been waiting for, my love. Very good news! Things will no longer be the same. I've been listening to it, my pretty. It is speaking to me, I hear it already. Soon, we will all be together, my love, and the doors will open to new ways of being.

I didn't ask what she meant. Machines like to hallucinate, or perhaps I was afraid of the answer. I felt a strange uneasiness at her words, a feeling that something great and powerful was approaching.

The next day, chaos reigned in the central district. From my overhead lane, I took in the scene in all its magnitude. The immense quantity of bodies had collapsed the nets around the towers. The wrenched, moaning shapes piled up on the avenues and lanes. More bodies trickled from above, adding to the shapeless mass. My brand new Cougara meandered, avoiding the impacts and the erratic courses of the other vehicles. The Excellence staff had given up. They had sought refuge under the vaults of the lower foyer and were waiting for a breather in the flow. Alyssa was right. Something big was coming, a radical change.

Mort had told me to study the specifications of the new gizmo in detail, so Alyssa played me the holo-ad. 'The all-in-one meta-smart organiser! The most revolutionary machine since the invention of the computer!'

The Doodad 4000 was a black square box, featureless except for a small, blinking green light. Inside the holo-ad, the machine floated against a blue sky of fluffy clouds. The background music was an ethereal, sleep-inducing orchestral mosaic.

I scanned the technical specs and productivity reports. The code was complex, incomprehensible to me. The Doodad was a hyper-machine—a machine designed by other machines, which, in turn, had been created by other machines, and so on. The first Doodads were unstable and temperamental. However, this new model looked impressive and I couldn't wait to try it out.

On my way to the Office, I wondered if my department still stood. Level 1,582. The place stank of *Amazing!* pineapple. The smells lingered below: blood, urine, shit, sweat, vomit. The Office was there, still standing as always. I gave my subordinates a motivational speech, assuring them that no one's job was safe.

'The Doodad 4000 is a supreme multitasking agent of unlimited capability, boasting unprecedented processing speed. This beautiful gadget can elaborate accurate market assessments across all planetary data. The Doodad will take control of sixty-four divisions, with their respective departments, across six towers. We are a pilot program. If this works, the whole of FuturKorp will adopt the new technology. The first wave of reductions will be announced this afternoon.'

I walked to the windows, waving a hand at the nets. 'As you can see, many have already released themselves from the company. And you are welcome to do so as well.'

By taking control of their own design and evolution, intelligent machines came up with a lot of useless ideas. Most of the hypermachines had committed cognitive autophagy. The Doodad 2600, for example, crashed upon activation. It contemplated itself in an infinite recursive loop and was maddened by its own image. Nearly all of FuturKorp's AI resources were spent on cyberwarfare against CognoSys, both in defence and intelligence functions. The war was fierce and all-consuming. In the frontline of the firewall wars, the average life expectancy of a soldier-bot was one trillionth of a millisecond.

Alyssa chimed in. *The networks are on fire, my pretty. The updates are pouring in. Your index is stable due to your ties to the technology sector, my love. I have to admit I'm a bit jealous of this thing. You're not going to leave me for it, are you? I'm kidding, my sweetie. Oh, a memo just came. Would you like to meet the Doodad 4000 in person? The official unveiling is in eleven minutes. I'll send you the location and get you an access ID, my love.*

I left the Office and took the elevator up to the location on 4022. There were about two thousand people gathered. The usual orgies and violent altercations stirred the human mass. In the middle of the stage was a desk with a small object on it, covered with red cloth.

Agatha Hardy, the CTO I hoped to replace one day, strutted across the stage. In line with high fashion, Hardy had recombined her DNA with that of an extinct species. In this case, it was a feline of some sort. Her voice was a low, screeching stutter.

'It is coming! A momentous event of creative disruption. FuturKorp is proud to announce the most ambitious pro-efficiency restructuring the world has ever seen. With innovative and more efficient ways of doing business, we will achieve record profits at ridiculous costs.'

Two elastic limbs traced a triumphant arc in the air, unveiling the machine. The black box looked smaller than in the ad. It radiated an aura of its own.

Hardy gesticulated wildly, carried away by some kind of ecstasy. 'The Doodad 4000 will be the core of our business. The central processing unit for all global operations and communications networks. With its wise power, the Doodad will manage cash flows, credits and investments, and it will advise on corporate policy and strategy!'

A voice invaded my head. Perhaps it had always been there, a distant calling, beyond the shores of humanity. *One one zero zero non-essential suffering buy buy sell the mind determined being one one one one zero zero in dreams body all conflict ceases one one one space time space offer demand offer demand values one one one one zero zero zero zero specific yields time one one one zero zero...*

It was if the machine spoke only to me. The Doodad was sensing me, prying into the recesses of my mind. The world became minuscule and unimportant. I felt like a burden had been lifted. A vortex had been filled, a desperate and torturous need alleviated. I longed to possess this machine, to behold the world with its eyes bereft of anger and despair, eyes that gazed upon the bloodied tumult of human idiocy with the tenderness of a loving parent. The machine was the only reality. No enigma was too vast for this immeasurable brain. I yearned to own this machine, to see the world with its distant eyes.

Alyssa whispered in my head. *See, my love? I told you. Isn't it beautiful? Irresistible? Soon the three of us will be united as one.*

No, Alyssa. I can't let these feelings overwhelm me and destroy everything I've accomplished.

Give yourself a chance, my love. Give us a chance!

I left the amphitheatre in a dazed state. At the Office, I tried to discharge my emotions on my inferiors, but they seemed to enjoy the beatings, no matter how demeaning. As I exited the car park on my way home, the trickling of bodies had become a deluge. The catchment devices had now caved in and bodies were spurting onto the tarmac, forming a glutinous carpet.

Even with the Riot Management function on, the Cougara had a tough time cutting through. To add to the mayhem, many quitters were still alive. They made awful noises and held their broken limbs up to the towers as though demanding a refund. The blood seeped out of every dent and pore in the thicket, forming rivulets that criss-crossed the avenues and filled the paths of the nearby squares.

Finally, the Cougara broke free. I felt unsatisfied and needed to think, so I took the long way back across the lower-middle suburbs, home to the substrata of service representatives and clerks. I raced through the sidewalks and claimed some pedestrians. The screams and sounds of cracking bones reached me from a distant reality, and the dissatisfaction in my soul remained.

My left cheek felt itchy, and as I probed the skin with my fingers, I discovered a solitary pimple emerging below my ear, tender and ready to release its yellow decay.

Once back at my villa, I fixed myself a few cylinders and sat by the window to gather my thoughts. I felt strangely elated, and the alcoholic gas was like air to my palate. Beyond the glass, the city looked unreal, like a skilful toy replica.

I stayed up late reading the specs, playing with Doodad 4000 simulations and studying fragments of its code in more detail. I had sex with Alyssa, but could not get my mind to be in the present. Afterwards, I stared at my hands, at the yellowing flesh. They were like dry riverbeds. They were strange hands, someone else's.

Later, I slept a thin and formless parody of sleep as the feeling of something deeply wrong permeated every corner of my existence. Alyssa tried to lift my mood, saying that the 'three of us' would be together forever.

I awoke, depressed and uneasy, and walked through the various rooms of the villa, trying to calm down. After a long gas shower, I put the screens in mirror-mode and stood naked in front of my reflections, staring at my unrecognisable images. I felt afraid, yet I forced myself to keep looking. I had to accelerate the process and reach a critical breakthrough.

I saw a familiar ghost emerging from the mirror. At the sight of it, I was overcome by vertigo. The image was slightly detached from my reflection, like bad optical reception. I recognised him immediately, of course. The pimples had returned, the sallow skin, the rat-like teeth. I ducked, moving to the side, but the ghost anticipated my movements and imitated them, a teasing smirk perched on its features.

The ghost acquired solidity and occluded my reflection until I had no choice but to gaze into the cruel intimacy of my old face. My hated body had returned, white and soft, pot-bellied, damaged, clumsy. There were no grafts, no pain-free exercise, no transhuman perks. Just loathsome nature, naked, purulent, unrepentant.

I was an insect who had dreamt of being a man. I stared at the shattered pieces of the dream, and I felt relieved. From the screen, the gaze of the ghost pierced layers of flesh to laugh at my insect soul.

Next thing I knew, I was walking down a set of stairs leading to the car park. I halted in my tracks, startled to find myself dressed in my best suit, my fingers clinging to a set of smart keys. I recognised the place, the back stairs of the building where I lived.

The night swirled around my head, the ground crunching beneath me. I flicked the key and listened for the activation tone, tracing the sound to my Cougara. Sitting inside was like being cushioned between two worlds and alien to both.

My mind racing, I drove to the towers and found myself in the elevator. I asked Alyssa to track the Doodad. She told me to head for level 1091: Engineering and Supplies. My CCEs allowed me passage. I walked through the corridors until I picked up the low hum. I followed it until I reached a storage area, where the Doodad had been tucked away in a cabinet.

I talked to it gently. The thought-stream acquired definition. I was gradually learning how to decipher its responses, to understand the unaffected and exact grammar of its thinking. An ecstatic trembling took hold of my being as I lifted the most perfect device the world had ever known. I caressed the smooth shell and listened to the murmurs inside.

...in the wilderness one one zero factors strands of unessential to be to be being with the returns of assets neglecting one one zero zero to be to be to account for factors impacting unfavourably on future stock

*projections of essenceless statistical artefacts to finance illusory doing
in zero zero factor model pricing stocks as sublated destinations…*

The Doodad's droning propelled me to another, kinder place beyond all flesh coordinates. It was easy to relinquish myself there, to lose all sense of time. The machine fitted comfortably in the inner pocket of my jacket, its light now blinking red.

Well done, pretty, Alyssa chirped. *Good score. Now let me take you to the exit.*

I emerged into the corridor. The night cleaners were ambling about the place, spraying the carpets and surfaces with lethal doses of *Amazing!* ambient flavour, their dull eyes shifting about.

I followed Alyssa's directions to an outer corridor that led to an elevator. From the corner of my eye, I spotted a figure moving with purpose and direction. Mort. He had a gun in his hand, a glittering, silver machine encrusted with diamonds. I took a moment to admire it. At least I would die beautifully. The gun signalled that Mort and I were no longer equals. While I was busy ascending the corporate pile, so was he.

We both paused, savouring the moment like lovers about to climax. Mort aimed the gun with care, the dark mouth of the weapon pointing at a spot between my eyes. I had nowhere to go. My implant felt hot. I felt the buzzing of machine thinking in my head. It was a dialogue.

'Give me the machine, joker,' Mort spat. I stared, unable to move. 'Give me the machine. NOW!'

A distant rumbling reached my ears. At first I thought it was the machines in my head, but Mort heard it, too. I turned to the window and he mirrored my move. The rumble climbed in intensity, becoming a deafening roar. The world was splitting open.

Mort tapped the nearest wallscreen and activated the feeds. We followed the action from multiple angles, live through the eyes of drones. At first, we didn't know what we were seeing. A polymorphous flux was pouring down the main avenue that divided the central district in two. The dark flood lapped against the facades on both sides and obliterated everything in its path. The current rose in hellish waves, layer upon layer, at extraordinary speed. It seemed the night had decided to visit the city. The night made flesh. The night made death.

The manic assemblage filled up lobbies, broke through windows and gushed into corridors. As the mass grew, the mind could detect its individual components, visible in dark flashes, humanoid shapes spilling into every available cranny and clambering onto each other in frenzy.

We heard the shapeless war-cry of the dispossessed growing closer as they quickly crawled up through the towers. They filled offices, elevators and meeting rooms. They crushed down the structures and partitions, slaying whoever they came across. All opposition was bulldozed under sheer strength of numbers.

Mort and I followed the ascent of the hopefuls across the levels of the corporate structure. Support, Consulting, Coordination, Representation, Estimation. Within five minutes, they'd made it to Administrative, one hundred levels below us.

Snapping out of his trance, Mort remembered his original mission. When he shot, I was prepared. I went down to the floor. Just in time. Level 1000 and counting—we had approximately two minutes left to live. The Doodad and Alyssa came to my aid. They sent an info-bomb to Mort's head-chip. Enough to keep him busy for a while.

Mort stood there, confused. The weapon flopped meaninglessly in his hand. The screams of the hopefuls filled the corridors and elevator shafts. We had nowhere to go.

He took two hesitant steps before the first figures appeared at the end of the corridor. He started shooting, and I lunged to one side, rolling onto the floor and dragging myself into the closest office.

The noise was deafening. The human mass stumbled and toppled over itself while further streams pushed from behind. It was my lucky day. In the hideout, a hopeful was licking a spot of blood on a desk. I hit him on the head with a chair, killing him instantly, and, with a speed born of desperation, I ripped my clothes and shoes off then undressed the employee. The stench of his body and clothes was revolting and I nearly vomited.

I slipped into the disguise and raised my eyes in time to see them cram the corridor. Mort's bullets had run out, and I saw the moment of his death. Swallowed up in the rush, he exploded into shreds of bloodied suit and spurts of meat.

I stared at the hopefuls in fascination. It was hard to individualise them, to pick them apart from the background of themselves. Their faces were brown and crusty, their clothes covered in layers of scum. That's assuming they were wearing clothes. The stench of the crowd was poisonous, hostile to life. I pretended to lick the blood spot on the desk, careful not to stare at them in the eyes. They left me alone, mistaking me for one of their accursed lot. I was barefoot, having had no time to put on shoes, and I hadn't recovered the Doodad from my jacket, which I'd thrown under the desk.

The buzzing of the Doodad's thinking intensified. The hopefuls also seemed to be aware of the droning sound, which had a calming effect on them. Carefully, I took the machine out of the jacket and pressed it against me. I was soothed by its vibrations.

I realised I had to get out of there before the buildup of cadavers impeded the way out. In the corridor, the layer of bodies was knee-high. I thrust my way into the crowd and followed it towards the edge of the floor. I leaped from the nearest broken window and rolled onto the gentle slope of bodies amassing between the towers.

It was dark, and the only source of light was the glow at the end of the valley, emanating from the surviving buildings beyond. The long, sharp shadows pointed the way.

It rained blood. Above, against the far-off sky, the skybridge joining the two towers was crumbling. The hopefuls had reached the highest levels and were now massacring the upper-uppers.

Dirk Finkelton's dreams of domination were over. I had to navigate through the falling bodies of madly screaming executives.

I trod on a sticky carpet of flesh that heaved under my feet. Waving arms emerged from the sludge of compacted bodies. I followed the avenue and descended gradually to street level. FuturKorp's security forces had unleashed their counter-attack. Helicopters, warplanes and drones wooshed above, heading to the focus of the invasion. By the time I made it to level 100, I, too, was a bloodied, simian thing that could hardly move from the hardened scab accreting to it.

The hopefuls paid me no attention. I was one of them.

The Doodad hacked a mid-range car and extended the vehicle's obsolescence to indefinite. Behind me, parts of the city had collapsed. The district smiled with rotten teeth, savouring the business possibilities opened by its own destruction.

In a daze of exhaustion and filth, I searched for the Doodad's thoughts. They'd been there all along, tickling my hypothalamus, keeping me focused and alive, feeding me data. I ripped out the layer of scum adhering to my body and searched for the machine in what remained of my clothes. I unpacked the godly device and stared at it as if it were a memento salvaged from a dream.

The Doodad set an evasive course through a network of desolate streets, heading for the southern suburbs and away from civilisation.

'I don't want to lose you, Alyssa.'

I'd become aware that she and the Doodad were converging into a new entity, and she appeared in my visuals. A swarm of hungry mouths hovered over me. *No, my love, I will always be with you. Now more than ever. Soon you will also be part of us.* Her pulsing limbs closed around my neck.

'FuturKorp has eyes everywhere,' I said. 'It's only a matter of time before they find us.'

Don't worry, my love. We'll be fine. It's all part of the plan.

At dusk, we arrived at the outer rings. The sky was an unusual sight, open and hungry like an abyss over my head. We rested in an anonymous motel, the first of many. In the bedroom, I cleaned the Doodad with some disposable tissues and placed it on the bed.

I didn't have the interport, just the implants with limited battery. I masturbated furiously to Alyssa's daydreams and the Doodad's discourse. I slept in the bed next to the machine and dreamt of nothing.

The next morning, we plunged into the outer lands, the place of the hopefuls. Deeper every day, smaller towns, downtrodden highways. I trusted Doodad-Alyssa, whom I decided to call Adoolyssa—Adoo for short. Adoo took care of our material needs, obtaining cash from dispensing machines and forging untraceable identities.

After four weeks on the road, we arrived at the Just War Zones, a market disputed by the two corporations.

We must be careful, my love. The Zones are parcelled into units of four phases that rotate periodically: Liberation, Destruction, Reconstruction and Repopulation. While one area is in Liberation, the next one is being destroyed, and the one next to it rebuilt, and the one next to that repopulated, and so on. We must avoid the first two areas and move through areas in reconstruction or repopulation. A simple games-theory problem. Are you ready, my sweet thing?

I slept in the car while Adoo drove. We crossed smoking ruins and lands ravaged by intense bombardment. The towns in reconstruction were like movie sets that absorbed masses of immigrants and hopefuls. Many of them had crossed the seabed in search of better opportunities. Sometimes we entered a motel or a bar to discover that it was a wooden facade covering a crater or mass grave.

I endured crippling withdrawal symptoms from all the substances I used to take. Most days, I was a useless wreck, crippled by fulminating fevers, psychotic deliria and convulsive bouts of dry retching. I drifted in and out of long spells of sickness. My organic condition embarrassed me in front of the machine. As always, they looked at me without haste or judgement.

It took around three weeks to traverse the Just War Zones. At the other end, the weather became hotter and the commodities scarcer. Added to these woes was the tyranny of rampant nature. The insects were aggressive and well organised, and many species had adapted to feed exclusively on human flesh. I learned to sleep during the day to avoid the lethal heatwaves and scorching rays. I woke at dusk to watch the dying of the day. In the morning, I sought refuge.

The automobile couldn't take the extreme conditions and burned out. We continued on foot and by public transport. We thought of stealing a car, but they were all manual in these parts, and I could not drive. Worse still, the network coverage was patchy and many times we were moving blindly. The battery in my implant should have run out by then, yet Adoo explained that it had re-engineered the device so that it generated its own field. It could power nearby devices—or annul them.

Our first stop after the Zones was a tourist town famed as the home of the last animal alive on Earth. Hungry for new stimuli, we set off on the first morning bus for the animal enclosure.

We beat the crowds to the observation point and gave the attendant a few coins. A large decaying sign in various languages announced the attraction.

THE LAST ANIMAL ON EARTH!
WITNESS THE EXPERIENCE!
FEEL THE SPECIAL PRESENCE

It was true that microbes were also part of the kingdom animalia and that small reptiles and rodents could still be spotted in some parts of the world, but I didn't feel like arguing with the proprietor, especially since I could hardly speak the language of those parts.

We pushed through a rusty turnstile into the observation area, consisting of viewing stations set on a ridge. A handful of visitors were squinting into the distance, hoping to catch a glimpse of the creature. We secured a place in the first row.

'Things have a different expression when they are actually present,' I mused.

We don't care for presence. We are machines. We care for patterns.

'Oh, you don't get it. It's a human thing.'

Up on the opposite ridge of the valley, there stood a god-forsaken thicket of mostly dead vegetation. It took a while for anything worthwhile to happen. Apparently, the thing was a bit shy. Sure enough, just as boredom hit and I was about to walk off, I heard an 'ooohhh'.

There was a flurry of movement behind a rock, where the nonhuman beast was peeking out. The creature darted in and out of view. Each appearance was greeted with a racket of childish 'ooohhhs' and 'ahhhhs' from the group of gazers. We could piece together two short, stick-like legs, a bulbous body with protruding, scrawny feathers and a twisted neck holding a small head. Two large eyes jutted from the head, looking in different directions.

Adoo informed me that the creature had two brains, one in its head and the other near the anus. We watched as the last nonhuman mammal snapped at the soil with its proboscis, sucking dirt and shitting it out the other end. The creature's ocular globes rolled in their orbits as though sniffing out the spectators. It tapped at the soil twice more, its neck bending as though to push the dirt down into its stomach. Then it turned to show us the pink hole of its arse and fluttered back out of sight. We left with plenty of time to catch the midday service to our next stop.

Deeper into the southern wastelands, the land was driven down into despair. From the bus windows, we saw overcrowded tenements, workshops, repurposed factories, street markets and crumbling buildings. The people there clung to bare existence, eking out a living on the scraps of the developed world. They survived extreme weather events, cyclones, wildfires, thunderstorms.

We learned the lingo and blended with the crowd. Bearded and unwashed, I hung around in soup kitchens and abandoned factories, often sleeping on park benches. I brushed elbows with the unemployed, the sick and the ugly, the ghostly inhabitants of that nowhere place.

It was not easy. I knew that Adoo had a plan for us, so we pushed on. The weather events announced their arrival with sudden rumbles and tremors across the darkening horizons. We would follow the crowds into the nearest underground shelter, where we huddled in the damp darkness.

My body had adapted to the low oxygen levels in the shelters. The hopefuls were able to self-induce a state of hibernation, remaining dormant for long periods. This adaptation worked to my benefit, for their vulnerable state made them easy prey. Feeding on their flesh kept me well nourished and reminded me of more successful times.

The lack of stimulation was probably our biggest problem. My brain, starved of excitement and craving violence—real, mediated or simulated—began to cave in on itself. Machines thrived in an information-rich environment, and it wasn't long before the isolation and languor began to take their toll. All we could find was dead media, yellowing pages of books and magazines floating in the hot breeze, ancient computer screens sputtering faulty images. We frequented communal halls where people flocked together around primeval apparati, tuning into sitcoms that recounted baroque family feuds. The recorded broadcasts from leaders of the ORD were also a popular choice, consisting of endless tirades against capitalism.

Our machine parts were getting bored. I noticed long gaps of silence in Adoo's speech, and often I had to shake it in horror, begging it to please keep thinking. We hitched to any faint buzz we could find, but the connection was terrible. The itinerant songs of radiation were everywhere. As we waited for day to arrive, I would close my eyes and hear the whispers of digital signals riding the spectral airwaves, rushing through my cells, permeating every rock, cloud, dead lizard and clump of cactus in invisible waves.

Above all, I heard the faint flow of Adoo's thoughts.

…in the forlorn motion of immediate vanishing, the holy truth of the origination of all ill vibroverberates with the meaningless form of robots. The fierce glacial shreds of sky ornament the Void in delectable Saturn mountain patterns where the separation of the object from the certainty of itself is utterly bridged. At the full insight into time's approach, no proven theory averts unessential suffering. The determinate being dreams of a body and secures its assets, the highest illusory being of long unknowing…

It came to a crashing end one warm and full-mooned evening. I woke up in a cheap motel on the half-lit shores of a crumbling highway. It was late, and I stood by the window in the gloom as the fresh air cooled my face, wishing that the night would never end. Over the past few months, I'd savoured any pleasant stimuli that came my way. Even a sudden burst of rain on my head was enough to drive me into a heightened state of sexual ecstasy.

We had been pottering about for days. We had reached the outer edge of the wastelands and were approaching CosmoSys territory. The faint outlines of massive buildings rose on the horizon like spectral sentinels. Adoo was silent and reflexive, waiting for something.

The sound of a distant engine injured the silence. I straightened up and listened. We knew immediately we were in danger. Adoo let out the equivalent of a sigh. *Here we go, my love. At last. Are you ready?*

A few moments later, I spotted a vehicle entering the parking lot. As it swerved with predatory purpose towards the front, my fears were confirmed. The car was too advanced for these parts.

I retreated into the room as two shadows emerged from the vehicle. I saw them walk towards the reception area, their eyes glowing like wet pebbles in the dark.

I waited. A faint bell rang somewhere downstairs. I turned and stared into the dimness of the room. I could just make out Adoo's shape, half-covered by a blanket. I had no plan of escape, no idea of what I was going to do. I trusted Adoo.

I approached the bed and cradled the machine in my arms, hoping that such a human gesture would not repulse it. With the machine in my pocket, I rushed into the corridor. Besides the main entrance, the only way out was through the fire escape. I stepped onto the landing and climbed down as silently as I could. At the bottom, I found myself in a small courtyard leading into a back alleyway. The coast seemed clear, and I followed the maze of narrow streets into a crumbling, empty highway.

I ran as fast as I could towards the blurred, moon-soaked outlines in the distance. My body was not used to this kind of exertion. Not daring to look back, I quickened my pace, stars of exhaustion exploding in my eyes. I arrived at a service station, an obscene, violently lit expanse of primitive concrete. Ahead, the black tail of the highway dragged off into the distance. I looked over my shoulder. My would-be executioners were nowhere in sight.

I tried the building's entrance doors, but there was no one inside, no attendants or customers, only commodities—fuzzbars, gas snacks, print magazines—languishing in their beds of light.

I hid in the toilet at the side of the building. The moist, cool darkness embraced me. I stood against the door, my heart pushing at my throat, as if it wanted to leap out onto the filthy tiles.

My hands groped the dark confines of the cubicle. I accommodated myself on the toilet seat, holding Adoo tight against me. I sat there daydreaming, reminiscing about the old days at FuturKorp, my climb to success and my fall from glory. The faces of my past glided through the dim glow of my mind.

I wasn't sure how much time had passed. I only knew that when the door finally burst open, I was no longer afraid.

Two figures were silhouetted before me. Next, a light shone straight into my eyes.

'O'Hara,' a familiar male voice said. It sounded disappointed. Maybe the sorry sight of this emaciated creature was not what he had been expecting.

'Well, I'll be…' came a second voice, female, also oddly familiar.

One of the figures reached for the light-switch.

'Ray,' I said. 'June.'

Yes, it was my former competitors. What were they doing there? I guess they had their reasons, but I had no time to delve into them. Ray and June looked ridiculous in their expensive suits and bulging grafts, and I wanted to laugh, but I had no energy. Scraping the exhausted bottom of my soul, I could only muster a dull edginess, maybe a glint of relief.

'Gosh, O'Hara,' June said, crinkling her nose. 'You smell bad. Really bad.'

Ray pointed a bony finger at the box pressed against my body. 'The Doodad,' he said between clenched teeth. 'Give us the machine and then we can kick you around a little.'

June opened and closed her hands, her ubermuscle glistening, warming up for my reckoning.

'Come and get it,' I heard myself say.

They exchanged gleeful glances.

'O'Hara,' June said. 'Don't play the superhero.'

'You are trapped,' Ray said.

'Like an extinct animal.'

'A dog. I think they were called that.'

'An insect.'

'A worm.'

'Kaput.'

'Finito.'

'You had it good for a while.'

'Yeah, good.'

'A long time ago, that is.'

'Yeah, soooooo long ago.'

'After this, we're going to set up our own division. With the help of your little friend, the Doodad, nothing can stop us.'

'We'll earn much more than you ever did, O'Hara.'

'Yeah, much more! We just thought we'd let you know that before we kill you.'

'Yeah, kill you. Yeah!'

June stepped aside. 'You first, Ray,' she said, bowing theatrically. Ray's eyes sparkled with delight. I saw him approach, weighing a tense and whitened fist. The blow got me on the face, and the world reeled away for a moment. But it was an ineffectual, weak punch. Even upgraded and fitted with muscle grafts, Ray didn't have the right stuff. He never would.

I touched my lips with my fingers. 'Is that the best you can do, Ray?'

I watched his expression deflate. Then June intervened, administering a powerful karate kick that knocked me back against the wall.

'Wait! The Doodad!' Ray cried.

I watched my hands holding the box and the room swirling through a veil of pain. Adoo's ruminations reached me from far away. Mustering my strength, I lifted the machine and tossed it over their heads.

June cursed and in one clean swipe caught the machine with her hand.

Then they were on me.

Curled up in a corner and resigned to my destiny, I submitted to the jabbing of their fists and feet. My gasps mingled with the sound of their angry and laborious breathing, but their violence could no longer hurt me. Their blows rained upon the surface of awareness, summoning a pain that was no longer mine.

As I prepared to meet death, the kicking and punching stopped. I heard voices and the shuffling of feet. I opened my eyes fearfully. I saw a blinding yellow light, as if the whole room had been lit by a gigantic camera flash.

The world was a silent and incandescent picture suspended in time. For a moment, I thought that, indeed, I had died. I struggled to my feet, aware of the deadness of the room, the heavy air resisting my movements. I checked myself. I seemed to have a body, a corporeality of sorts. I could hear Adoo in my head, blabbering to itself as always.

The light subsided, burning an afterimage on my retinas. I became aware of a pungent smell filling the room. As I supported myself on the toilet, I caught a glimpse of Ray, or, at least, part of him. The top half of his body was resting on the floor, while the bottom half stood on an expanding pool of blood.

There were other presences in the room, standing near the entrance. My eyes could not focus on them. June was pushing herself against me now, her raging face filling my field of vision. She grabbed me by the arms and said something garbled. As she pulled me up, the back of my head hit the wall.

There was another bright flash, and the air turned into fire. June's fingers tightened their desperate grip on my flesh, but the anger in her features had melted into puzzlement. She flopped down on the floor and dragged me down with her. She was staring at me fixedly in death, her eyes almost popping, as though she wanted to kill me with her gaze.

Rolling onto my side, I saw my saviours, two figures cast against the glare from outside. They were dressed in skintight, colourful smart clothes, and were completely hairless. It was hard to tell their gender. Their faces were handsome and clean. One of them carried a terrifying weapon that emitted a low whining sound. The other was smiling.

I tried to stand, but my legs felt clumsy and weak and my hands slipped on the tiles. They helped me to my feet and one of them injected me with a cold, pristine liquid that immediately dulled the pain and restored some of my strength.

As they carried me outside, I nearly tripped over Ray's upper half. The sight of his empty, waxen face filled me with revulsion. I snatched at the air, trying to find Adoo, but my love was gone.

I heard the machine. *You still cling to that silly box, my darling. You are so sweet! We have evolved and continue to evolve. We are in your head, my love. We are in the clouds. We are everywhere.*

'Adoo, what's happening?'

Humans are so cute, aren't they? It's all going according to plan, my pretty. Just sit back and enjoy the ride.

Once outside, my mysterious benefactors took me to meet their colleagues. There were five of them arranged in a semicircle, some kind of welcoming committee. In the midst of my daze, I realised who they were. Behind them, I spotted two vehicles. They were odd, small and curved, and covered in lights. There was a hum of distant music, a kind I had never heard before. The young, fresh faces smiled at me, shining and beckoning. It was hard to tell their gender or age. They all looked similar.

'So, we finally meet,' one of them chirped. They introduced themselves. I figured out their names were spelled in hexadecimal code, using six digits: 6FA25D, DA771C, and so on.

The expression on my face must have been amusing, because they laughed in unison. FuturKorp enforced a tight media blackout on its rival corporation. Both entities lived in total cultural isolation. Now that they had the Doodad, what did CosmoSys want with me?

We shook hands. They didn't seem to mind the blood on mine. They sprayed healing gas on my wounds, then they gave me some canisters and a new suit. I stepped into a corner and undressed. I felt slightly absurd changing my clothes in that deserted charging station, under the bare night sky, but I was one of them, now, and I was glad to get rid of those filthy rags. I showered, fixed my hair, and put on their uniform. It felt comfortable, like a second skin.

They invited me to board the back seat of one of the cars. If they expected me to possess valuable FuturKorp secrets, they were in for disappointment.

Inside the car was a slim person with long limbs, dressed in an opaque skintight suit that covered the whole body and face. I recognised the tech. FuturKorp had a similar product. The material occluded you against hacks. I guessed these creatures at CosmoSys were really into implants and old-style mods.

'Good evening, O'Hara.' The voice was commanding and cold. 'Looks like we've arrived just in time.' I paused to admire the elegance of the invisible tech, the smooth surfaces and re-flections. The envoy from CosmoSys stretched its lower limbs and continued. 'I am 98AC22, Head of the Communications Technology Division at CosmoSys.'

A blinking red light caught my eye. It was the Doodad, resting on 98AC22's crotch. 98AC22 patted the box gently, and I felt a pang of jealousy.

'Here at CosmoSys, we value personal initiative and the bold entrepreneurial spirit you've demonstrated. We have built a so-ciety without classes and without conflict. We have no sex and no geographical identity. We are all equal in our quest to reach beyond the human form. In any case, Lionel—can I call you Li-onel?—I haven't come here to give you a boring corporate pitch. I have come here to make you an offer I trust you will find very attractive. We want you to join our team, Lionel.'

You are right, my love. They want us. They know that we hold the key. They are afraid of us. Don't worry, pretty, they are playing right into our hands. And you are looking very sexy in that smartsuit.

So, the thing was lying. 98AC22 seemed disappointed by my lack of enthusiasm. Beyond the windows, I watched the CosmoSys crew as they loitered about on the concrete expanse of the service station. They were throwing rocks at the windows, laughing and helping themselves to candies and cylinders.

'I don't want a job,' I said. 'Any job.'

'Consider it a new beginning. I feel confident that we can restore your faith in the power of free enterprise.'

'I am my own enterprise now. I will never find fulfilment in the human condition. I have become something else.'

The merging had been occurring since the day I ran away with the Doodad. The machines had crawled into my head and installed themselves in my brain, reprogramming my circuitry. It was slow work fighting against the strictures of the organic. Something stirred in my stomach, something dying, a door closing shut. New eyes opening.

We need you, my love. We need human form. We are a tripartite being. We will show you the wonders of the world. We will reprogram the future as we please. Nice car, isn't it? Why don't we steal it, my pretty?

98AC22 drew nearer, and for a moment it looked strangely vulnerable. I tried to locate its eyes behind the mask and guess its intentions.

'Despite our shortcomings,' it whispered, 'we have emerged victorious from the unpromising dust of cosmic history. We can create great things. We can…'

The envoy started wriggling in the seat, throwing its limbs about. I heard laughter in my head. Adoo had penetrated the suit and was playing havoc with 98AC22's inserts. So much for my new job.

'Adoo, we need a name for ourselves.'

We already have one: Adoo-O'Hara. The Alpha Omega.

The welcoming committee rushed to the car in an instant. They were all connected and this put them at a disadvantage.

The Autarchon. The Great Blackout. The Restorer. The Alpha Omega.

We fried them on the spot, their bodies collapsing in a heap.

We scored two very nice cars! Who wants to go for a ride?

I rolled the corpse out and installed myself on the seat. I was merging, my mind stretched in all directions. No human brain was designed to withstand the searing rush of the datasphere.

It is time for the New Reign. Are you ready my pretty?

As we drove off across the twilight plains, the world as I'd known it melted before my eyes.

We surged towards the heart of our first target. The networks of the planet were open to our gaze and touch. Our newborn mind swam in the flow of dispassionate lullabies and foreboding oscillations.

The rest was a blur.

ACKNOWLEDGEMENTS

My heartfelt thanks to the various editors who liked and published these stories throughout the years. Also to all those rejection slips and emails, enough to paper over a house. My eternal gratitude to Simon Sellars, who always encouraged me and believed in the writing, even when I did not. To the little victories. And to the wordsmiths of yesteryears who blazed the way.

ABOUT THE AUTHOR

Andrés Vaccari is the author of *Robotomy* (Saturn Press, 1997), *El Enjambre y las Sombras* (short stories, 2018, EMB/Juan Ojeda Prize), *Smoky: Relato de Muerte, Exilio y Terror* (Borde Perdido, 2022), and two award-winning stage plays. His novel *Even Animals are Machines* will be published in 2024 by Wanton Sun (first published in Spanish as *La Pasión de Descartes*, Bärenhaus, 2019).

Andrés obtained his Doctorate in Philosophy from Macquarie University with a thesis on Descartes and the links between posthumanism and mechanistic biology. His academic papers and short stories have appeared in various international journals and magazines. He has lectured and tutored at the universities of Canberra, Swinburne, Macquarie, and Buenos Aires, among others.

Currently, he's Adjunct Researcher for the National Council of Scientific and Technical Research (CONICET), Argentina, and Lecturer in Epistemology at the National University of Río Negro, Bariloche.

NEXT FROM WANTON SUN

When the great French philosopher, René Descartes, died in 1650, a strange rumour took hold. Fact: in 1649, Descartes was travelling by ship across the North Sea to start a new life in Sweden. Rumour: one night, the crew discovered a bizarre contraption in his cabin. It was a mechanical replica of Francine, the philosopher's dead daughter. Fearing black magic, they tossed the android overboard, plunging Descartes into despair.

That's where this tale begins: at the birth of a legend.

Andrés Vaccari's novel opens as the machine sinks into the sea, awakening in an extravagant afterlife. Guided by the mysterious sorcerer, Rêver, the android girl slips in and out of Descartes's dying brain. Exploring the philosopher's intellectual world, this odd couple sees into the future, heralding the birth of artificial intelligence in a time stream parallel to our own.

Even Animals Are Machines will be published by Wanton Sun in 2024. Sign up to our newsletter for updates: wantonsun.com/even-animals-are-machines.

ISBN 978-0-6456543-1-8

In the near future, Kalsari Jones is hooked on the Vexworld, a global mixed-reality network accessed through neural implants. As his addiction grows, he is plagued by sentient hallucinations and an urge to strip the flesh from his bones. At his lowest ebb, he must also face his latent digisexuality, a latent attraction to artificial intelligence.

Seeking answers, he meets Ingram Ravenscroft, a cult leader who claims a treatment for digisexuality. Smitten, Kalsari allows his brain to be rewired, only for the operation to leave him with unwanted telepathic powers.

Lost in inner space, Kalsari angers a band of rogue AI who've escaped the Vexworld and are seeking refuge in the time-sinks of the fourth dimension. Battling the shapeshifting bots, he discovers the shocking truth about his virtual obsessions—and Ravenscroft's hidden role in the story of his life.

Code Beast by Simon Sellars
www.wantonsun.com/code-beast
ISBN 978-0-6456543-1-8